ROMANCE

**Large Print Ste
Steele, Jessica.
Married in a moment**

MARRIED IN A MOMENT

MARRIED IN A
MOMENT

BY

JESSICA STEELE

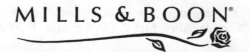

First published in Great Britain 1998
Large Print edition 1998
Harlequin Mills & Boon Limited,
Eton House, 18-24 Paradise Road,
Richmond, Surrey TW9 1SR

© Jessica Steele 1998

ISBN 0 263 15751 2

Set in Times Roman
16-9810-56941 C16-16½

Printed and bound in Great Britain
by Antony Rowe Ltd, Chippenham, Wiltshire

CHAPTER ONE

ELLENA stared at the television screen in stunned horror, her brain numbed by what the newscaster had just announced—an avalanche in the Austrian Alps. An avalanche in the very area where Justine was spending a ski-ing holiday with her boyfriend Kit!

Ellena didn't seem able to think as the newscaster carried on solemnly about tons of snow, rocks and boulders, and no chance of anyone surviving such circumstance! Having done with that piece of news, he went on to the next item.

Though still disbelieving, she was starting to recover sufficiently from her initial shock to tell herself that she was panicking unnecessarily. Only that morning she had received an 'our hotel'-type of picture postcard from her sister... But—that must have been posted days ago!

Hurriedly Ellena found the card, feverishly scanning it and looking to see if by any chance there was a printed hotel telephone number. There was! In next to no time she was busy dialling. If she could just speak to Justine...

5

The line was engaged. For a half-hour the line was engaged. Ellena accepted that she was not the only anxious relative wanting to get through, though the waiting was unsustainable.

Perhaps Justine was trying to get through to her. She would know that Ellena would be anxious. She put her phone down. It did not ring.

All lines were probably swamped anyway. Perhaps Kit had managed to get through to his family. He had two brothers; the middle one, Russell, and his wife, Pamela, were looking after their baby while Justine and Kit were away.

Ellena was enormously thankful that she'd insisted on having Russell's address in Hertfordshire and phone number before Justine left. Ellena had never met any of Kit's family, but—interfering though it might be, or perhaps because she was so used to looking out for Justine—she had already phoned once to see if baby Violette was settled without her mother. Pamela, Russell's wife, had been more than a shade frosty, she recalled. But Ellena cared not for Pamela Langford's frostiness just now and, finding the number, she dialled.

'Hello, Russell. Ellena Spencer—J-Justine's sister.' Striving to keep calm, she announced herself—and hesitated, suddenly realising that if he had not had a telephone call from Kit, nor had he been watching the news, she was going to have to break the news to him herself.

But, 'Bad do,' he replied, and she knew that he was aware of the avalanche.

'You haven't heard anything from Kit? He hasn't phoned or anything?' she questioned urgently.

'We had a card from him this morning, but that's all.'

'Oh,' Ellena cried faintly, starting to feel a shade frantic. 'I've tried to phone the hotel, but I can't get through.'

'Try not to worry. Pamela says you'll hear soon enough if Kit and your sister are involved.' Russell attempted to soothe her, and she wondered how they could be so passive. Not worry...! 'According to the news report we were watching, that area was out of bounds— there shouldn't have been anyone in that area.'

Oh, heavens! Ellena was two years older than Justine and had done her best to take care of her when their parents had been killed in a mountaineering accident five years ago. Ellena knew from experience that anything labelled 'out of bounds' was a magnet for Justine. There shouldn't have been anyone in the avalanche area! When had that ever stopped Justine?

'I think I'll keep trying to get through to the hotel,' she stated, starting to feel torn. If she went to her office and sent a fax there'd be no one at her flat to take any incoming call. 'If Kit rings you, would you…?'

'Look, if you're seriously worried, why not ring Gideon? He'll know how to get through.'

Gideon Langford was the eldest of the three brothers. By all accounts he was successful in everything he did, a high-flyer making the engineering firm started by his father into the vast empire it was today. Popular with the opposite sex—but light on his toes, apparently, when it came to marriage talk.

All the same, it defeated her to know how he could get through to the hotel if she couldn't. But she was beginning to feel quite desperate. Desperate enough to try anything. 'Have you got his number?' she asked.

Ellena tried the hotel again first, but when she again couldn't get through she dialled the number Russell had given her. It was engaged, as it was on her second and third attempt. On her fourth attempt, however, it rang out, and was answered.

'Langford!' an all-male voice answered abruptly. So abruptly, Ellena just knew that her call was most unwelcome.

'I'm sorry to bother you—' then no more for-
mality; she was almost past caring whom she
bothered '—my name's Ellena Spencer—I'm
Justine's sister.'

'Justine?' he demanded clarification.

'Justine and Kit, your brother,' she inserted,
too het up to feel foolish, because he'd know
Kit was his brother, for goodness' sake!
'They're on a ski-ing holiday together and—'

'You've heard the news?' Gideon cut in
tersely, clearly a man who had little time to
waste.

'About the avalanche. Yes,' she said. 'I've
been trying to get through to the hotel, but—'

'They're missing!' he stated shortly.

'Missing?' she gasped. How Gideon
Langford had come by that information totally
irrelevant as she clutched hard onto the phone
receiver.

'My brother and his companion left their hotel first thing this morning—they haven't been
seen since.'

'Oh, no!' she whispered, tears springing to
her eyes. 'They might have gone anywhere,' she
choked, clutching at straws. 'Russell said that
the area of the avalanche was out of bounds.'

Gideon Langford took in that she had been in
touch with his other brother without comment-

ing on it. 'Did he also tell you Kit would merely see that as another rule to be broken?' he snarled harshly.

'J-Justine and Kit are—well met,' Ellena answered, her voice starting to fracture, the realisation hitting her that Gideon Langford's harshness might stem from the fact he was keeping a lid on his own emotions about his youngest brother. 'Is that all you know?' she questioned.

'I'll find out more when I get there.'

'You're going to Austria to—?'

'I'll have a plane standing by in a couple of hours,' he butted in grimly. Then he paused for a moment and, still in the same grim tone, asked, 'Do you want to come?' He didn't sound very enthusiastic.

'Yes,' she answered without hesitation—it didn't require any thinking about.

'Where are you?'

'My flat near Croydon.'

'Your address?' he demanded, barely before she had finished speaking. She gave it to him. 'I'll send a car. Be ready in an hour,' he instructed, and rang off.

An hour ago she'd been watching the television. Now she was on her way to Austria! At any other time she might have taken exception to Gideon Langford's bossiness. But not now.

At this moment she was only grateful that he was taking charge. She felt a desperate need to be near Justine. Anything was better than sitting at home worrying.

As instructed, she was ready an hour later when a chauffeur-driven limousine arrived to take her to the airport.

And it was at the airport, in a private waiting area, that she caught her first glimpse of the man who ran that mammoth concern, Langford Engineering—Kit's brother! Gideon Langford was tall, about ten years older than Kit, well over six feet, dark-haired and, as they shook hands, she felt pinned by a direct look from his unwavering slate-grey eyes.

She felt herself being checked over, starting with her straight blonde hair, now held back in a neat chignon. Then his eyes took in her creamy skin, her slightly hollowed cheeks and photogenic high cheekbones that ˙ sometimes caused her to seem aloof. She wasn't particularly aloof, she didn't think. It was just that she usually had some problem on her mind—most often something to do with Justine.

'I don't suppose you've heard any further news?' she enquired, as he let go of her hand.

He shook his head. 'We'll just keep hoping,' he said shortly, and that was about the sum total of their conversation until someone came to show them to the private jet.

They had little to say to each other throughout the journey, either. While she knew Gideon Langford was busy with his own thoughts, Ellena lapsed into thinking of her years with Justine since their parents' deaths. They had been killed on a mountainside—she couldn't bear it if Justine, too, perished... No, no, she wouldn't think that way; she just wouldn't.

She had been just seventeen; Justine fifteen—and on the point of being expelled from school for some misdemeanour. Which of her misdemeanours it had been exactly was lost under the weight of all the others when word had reached them of their parents' accident.

They had both been much loved by their lively, bubbly parents, but Ellena had had to do some instant growing up. Prior to the accident, she had been hopeful that her father, as he had before, might have been able to persuade Justine's school from taking such drastic action as expulsion. But, he didn't come back and, while they were both devastated at losing their parents, it was Justine who had adored her father—he who, it had to be said, had indulged her endlessly and had refused to see anything wrong in a few high spirits and who had been inconsolable for months.

During this time Ellena had realised that her plans to go to university to study accountancy were not going to happen. Although in the light of the tragedy the school had relented, and allowed a much subdued Justine to stay with them, Ellena had felt there was no way she could leave her.

Hiding her own heartache, she'd set about the practicalities of living without their parents. Out of necessity she'd checked into their financial security.

Their finances weren't brilliant, but they weren't too bad either, she'd discovered. Both she and Justine were aware of an investment which their father had made for them both in the years of their birth. They would each receive a quite substantial amount—but not until their twentieth birthdays.

Meantime, their parents' house was heavily mortgaged and there were a few dcbts outstanding; they had all lived well, but there was nothing left over for a rainy day.

Ellena had left school straight away and, excelling at maths, obtained a job with a firm of accountants. She was reasonably well paid for her junior position, but it was nowhere near enough to pay the mortgage.

'The house has got to go. Do you mind very much?' she'd told Justine gently.

'Without Mummy and Daddy here—I don't care at all,' Justine had replied listlessly.

'We'll find a lovely flat to rent,' Ellena had decided with a brightness she was far from feeling.

'If that's what you want...'

It wasn't, but facts had to be faced. So the house had been sold—with just enough money left over to settle all bills and, Ellena hoped, pay rent—if they were careful for the next three years—until her twentieth birthday when she could claim the money from her father's investment.

Justine had not cared for the first four apartments they'd looked at, but had started to perk up when Ellena, trying not to despair, found a flat at the more expensive end of the market.

'The rent's a bit more than I'd calculated.' Ellena had thought it wouldn't hurt to let Justine know there would have to be a few economies.

'I'll leave school and get a job too,' Justine had declared.

'I think we can manage while you finish your education,' Ellena had smiled, and, because

Justine was just Justine, she'd given her a loving hug. Justine had clung to her.

It had been a wrench for Ellena to leave the rambling old house she had been brought up in, but, with more than enough furniture to spare, she and Justine had moved into their new home and started to try to rebuild their lives.

On the plus side, Justine had begun behaving herself at school, and, joy of joys, Andrea Keyte, the head of A. Keyte and Company, the accountancy firm Ellena worked for, had called her into her office one wonderful morning. Mrs Keyte, then a divorced lady of thirty-seven, had interviewed her personally for the job, so knew all about her present qualifications, and that she had hoped to study accountancy. Mrs Keyte had, she'd said that wonderful morning, observed how much Ellena enjoyed her work and how easily she seemed to grasp complicated issues. How, she'd enquired, would Ellena feel about being articled to her?

'You mean—train to be an accountant—to gain my qualifications here?' Ellena gasped, suddenly starting to see light, unexpected, wonderful light, after the darkness of recent months.

Apparently, that was exactly what Mrs Keyte—who was later to invite Ellena to call her Andrea—did mean. 'It will mean a lot of hard work,' she cautioned. 'Study in the evenings when you'd probably much rather be out with your boyfriend.'

Ellena didn't have a boyfriend. What time did she have? Before her parents' deaths she'd spent evenings and weekends either swotting over homework from school, or on some mad adventure with them. Since their deaths, Justine had taken precedence.

'I can do it,' she said eagerly. 'I *know* I can do it.'

'It will take all of five years for you to be ready to take your finals,' Andrea had warned.

'I want to do it; I really do.' Ellena, fearful that her employer might change her mind, promised this earnestly.

'Then you shall.'

And she had. It had not been easy. Left alone to cope with the work and the studying, Ellena knew she would have coped with only minor panics. But, in avowing, 'I *know* I can do it', she had not taken Justine—or rather Justine finally coming to terms with the loss of their parents—into consideration.

By the time Justine's sixteenth birthday had approached, it seemed she was close to being expelled from school again.

'I'd better find time to go and see if your headmaster will overlook your truancy one last time,' Ellena stated when, having arrived home from the office with a load of studying to do, Justine owned up to not having been to school for a while.

'I shouldn't, if I were you,' Justine grinned, 'I've no intention of going back—even if they'd have me.'

'Justine!'

'Don't go on, there's a love. I've been awfully good today.'

Ellena did not trust the word 'good'. ' "Good", as in...?'

'As in, I've been and got myself a job in a boutique. I start tomorrow.'

'You're not sixteen yet!' Ellena gasped.

'I told them I was. And I will be, by the time they find out I wasn't.' She laughed. She was infectious. Ellena remembered she had laughed too.

Dear, dear Justine, she couldn't be dead! Ellena choked on a sob of sound, and caught Gideon Langford's sharp glance on her from across the aisle. She hastily turned to look, unseeing, out of the aircraft window at the night sky.

He looked pretty bleak too, she realised, and strangely felt she wanted to help his suffering in any way she could. She realised her sensitivities at this dreadful time must be bouncing about all over the place, and strove again to calm her emotions. She had no idea what lay before them—it could be the best or the worst of news—so she must gather what strength she could.

Determinedly she pushed the weakening worst thoughts from her. Concentrate on the good things, she instructed herself. That time Justine... Her thoughts were at once back with Justine: Justine laughing, Justine crying; Justine bringing her first boyfriend home, the great unwashed group of her friends who had—to the dismay of their neighbours—almost camped on their doorstep; Justine starting new jobs, lasting a day, a week—miracle of miracles one job had even lasted three months! Justine's taste in boyfriends improving—her boyfriends starting to look as though they bathed and changed their clothes regularly.

By the time Ellena was twenty, and their finances were at last buoyant, however, she'd had enough of chasing halfway around London on what transport she could find, looking for Justine when she didn't come home at night.

Ellena had found time to have driving lessons, and bought a car. She'd had many qualms about letting Justine have driving lessons as well—she was hard enough to keep tabs on. But, as ever, her soft heart had won over her sensible head, and Justine learned to drive too—and Ellena bought her a car also. Then Justine fell in love—and the man she fell in love with seemed equally fluffy-minded.

Kit Langford wasn't too keen on work either, by the sound of it. 'What does he do?' Ellena had asked.

'Do?' Justine seemed to have no idea what she meant. 'Oh, you mean *work*! Oh, he's not working at the moment; he's having too good a time spending the money he came into on his twenty-first birthday from his father's estate.'

Ellena was sorry that Kit was without a father too. But she couldn't help but feel responsible for her younger sister. 'Does he live at home with his mother?' she asked.

'His mother remarried a year after his father died—she's living somewhere hot—the Bahamas, I think.'

'So where does he live?'

'He's got a flat; his brother bought it for him when he booted him out of his house.'

'His brother...'

'Well, it was rather a riotous party, and Gideon was away. But we did try and clear up all the mess.'

Justine had no need to go on. Ellena saw the picture quite clearly. She had herself come home from a late evening office function one time to find all hell had been let loose in her absence—music blaring and all sorts of people, no two with hair the same colour—pinks and greens all competing. Justine had decided to have a party. It had taken all of a week to restore the flat to good order, and a month to be on speaking terms with the neighbours again.

When Justine had fallen in love with Kit, though, no one else seemed to exist for her but him. Gradually Ellena had learned a little more about Kit's family. They were well to do, by all accounts, though Justine had never met either of his brothers. Kit saw his eldest brother occasionally, and there were frequent phone calls between the two, but Gideon Langford had a busy life on all fronts. Kit, who seemed as besotted with Justine as she was with him, wanted to spend all his time with her.

They had been going out with each other for quite some while when, as happy as you please, Justine had come home, holding a bottle of champagne aloft.

Ellena had broken off from her studies. 'We're celebrating?' she teased, joy in her heart that, by the look of it, her little sister had just become engaged.

She should, she'd later realised, have known not to prejudge anything where Justine was concerned. For, grinning madly, and obviously delighted, 'We're pregnant!' she announced.

Ellena was studying hard for her finals just then, though, had she thought that being pregnant might calm Justine down to lead a quieter life, she discovered she was much mistaken—Justine's relationship with Kit entered a stormy phase. And while Ellena had been mentally adjusting to the fact that her sister might soon be leaving to set up home with Kit—of that there had been no sign.

Justine still met Kit occasionally, but, more often than not, would come home needing to be soothed. When Ellena wasn't calming Justine's agitation, she was coping with her being unwell—and wondering what to do for the best. Her tenancy agreement stated definitely, no children. By the look of it, they would have to find somewhere else to live.

Then everything seemed to be happening at once. Ellena took her final accountancy exam—and with joy and not a little astonish-

ment learned she had passed with an exceptionally good mark. But, even while she was
relaying this news, Justine went into labour.

'I want Kit!' she'd cried.

Ellena contacted him and was warmed by his
caring. He must have broken all records—he
was at the hospital only minutes after Justine
and Ellena—she didn't know which of the three
of them was the more panic-stricken.

Kit stayed with Justine when the time arrived,
and Ellena paced the waiting area fearing she
was going to break down in tears and disgrace
herself at any moment now if she didn't hear
something soon.

Then Kit, his grey look gone, grinning from
ear to ear, was coming to find her. 'What do
you think of Violette Ellena?' he asked—and,
uncaring that she might disgrace herself, Ellena
waited only for him to add that mother and
daughter were doing fine before she burst into
tears.

She had thought Kit seemed to grow up a
little then. In any event he wouldn't hear of anything, other than Justine and their daughter moving in with him. In the short time Justine was
in hospital he turned his sparc bedroom into a
baby's room, complete with crib and fluffy toys.

Justine was the happiest Ellena had ever seen her. She was but a few weeks away from her twentieth birthday. 'You feel all right about moving in with Kit?' Ellena felt she had to ask. 'You needn't. If you're worried about our tenancy agreement, we can look for...'

'I'm very all right about it,' Justine answered, and it was clear that such a small thing as having a landlord come down on them like a ton of coals for breaching their tenancy agreement had never for one moment bothered her. 'I want to live with Kit.'

'In that case, since you'll have enough to do looking after the baby, I'll pack your clothes and—'

'No need to bother with that, Ellena-Ellen,' Justine interrupted sweetly, using a pet name for her sister she always used whenever everything in her world was rosy. 'It'll take a little while for me to get my shape back, I expect, so I'll have to manage with a couple of these tents you bought me! But, as soon as my inheritance comes through, I intend to dump my old wardrobe and buy new clothes.'

In Ellena's view, Justine had some lovely garments in her wardrobe and it would be a sin to throw them out. But Justine had just been a very brave girl, and had presented her with a most beautiful little niece. Justine could do no wrong. Even when, as the weeks went by, she spent money like it was going out of style.

Kit had a single bed fitted into the minute box-room in his flat. It came in useful when, more and more frequently of late, they asked Ellena to come and baby-sit her niece.

Ellena had babysat the adorable scrap a week ago last Saturday evening. But it was on Sunday morning, as she was preparing to return to her own home, that she learned that Justine was as irresponsible now as she ever had been.

Ellena said goodbye to Kit, cooed a 'bye-bye' to the wonderful little girl who had so soon won her heart, and was about to make her farewells to her sister when Justine said she'd come out to her car with her.

Oh, dear, knowing her of old, Ellena suspected Justine had something to say which she feared she might not like to hear. She'd had an hour in which to say something—yet she was leaving it until Ellena was on her way out!

'We're going away tomorrow,' Justine announced as they walked to the parking area. 'We'll—er—probably be away for a month or so.'

Given that it was January, and had seemed a long winter, a month somewhere warm might do them all the world of good. 'Where are you going?' she asked, her thoughts on Violette and how they would have to guard her. 'You don't think you should wait until the baby's a little older?' she queried. She didn't want to put a damper on their plans but, apart from the time factor, and what would be involved in getting any vaccinations done—wasn't Violette a little young for such treatment?

'Oh, we're not taking her with us!' Justine answered blithely. While Ellena was starting to be concerned that there was no way she could look after baby Violette for 'probably a month or so' and at the same time do her job, Justine was going on: 'Kit's heard of this wonderful place in the Austrian Alps. We're going ski-ing. And don't worry, Kit's brother's going to mind the baby while...'

'His brother! Gideon? The one who, according to reports, works all day and parties all night?' Ellena exclaimed aghast.

'No, not him! Kit's other brother.'

Ellena was only marginally relieved. 'Russell, the married one?'

'Mmm, Russell,' Justine confirmed. 'Kit hasn't seen him in ages, and he's a bit of a dream—while his wife, Pamela, she's a bit of a shrew, with a nose for money like no one you've ever met! When I mentioned I'd be pre-pared to pay handsomely—and for the cost of a temporary nanny—she couldn't offer her ser-vices fast enough.'

Apparently Kit had used up all the money left to him by his father. But Ellena didn't think she liked the sound of this arrangement at all. Perhaps she could employ a temporary nanny herself to take care of the baby during the day and look after her herself at night. But compli-cations stirred before she could so much as voice her thoughts. Apart from the fact that chil-dren were not allowed where she lived—crying babies with massive lung power in particular—since qualifying as an accountant she was start-ing to take responsibility for her own clients; hers was no longer a nine-to-five job.

'But—but—what about clothes?' She was putting obstacles in the way on purpose, she knew she was, but somehow she couldn't bear the thought of them going away and leaving the baby with strangers.

'Oh, heck, Ellena, I've put on an inch or two since Violette arrived; my old salopettes were never going to fit me anyway. Besides, what are credit cards for?'

By the sound of it Justine, who was still replenishing her wardrobe, intended to purchase all she required at her holiday destination.

Ellena knew she was on a losing argument, even as she suggested, 'Don't you think Violette's a little young to be left with strangers? She's only…'

'Oh, Ellena!' Justine exclaimed impatiently. 'I knew you'd be like this, which is why I didn't tell you straight away when Kit and I decided to take off. Besides, Violette has met Russell and Pamela—we went there one day last week when we were wondering who best to leave her with. Ideally it would be you, but you're going up in the world with your job and, having wrecked your social life over the years—I know I've been sheer murder for you sometimes,' she put in, her flare of temper dying as she became loveable, charming Justine again, 'I just didn't want to be responsible for wrecking your career so soon after you've qualified.'

'Oh, Justine!' Ellena said helplessly.

'Austria's not the moon,' Justine smiled winningly.

That had been the last time she had seen her. How glad she was now that she had asked for Pamela and Russell Langford's address and phone number, that she and Justine had said goodbye on friendly terms. She had managed to wish her a happy holiday, Ellena recalled—and without realising it, took a shaky breath.

'We're about to land,' the stern-faced man sitting across the aisle cut into her darkening thoughts.

'Thank you,' she mumbled, made hastily aware that she was in an aircraft and that in the next hour or so she could be hearing news that she did not want to hear.

Icy cold air hit them as the plane door opened. Ellena was glad of her thick trousers, sweater and sheepskin coat. Glad, too, of Gideon Langford's assistance because, for all he didn't seem to say much, and what he did say was curt and to the point, it was he who made what explanations were necessary. He took over, asking questions—though there was no more news now than there had been then.

She had brought only the barest minimum in the way of luggage, and without humour wondered if perhaps she was more like her younger sister than she realised.

But then Ellena discounted this, realising that, unlike Justine, her reasons were practical. Gideon Langford had said, 'I'll have a plane standing by', so she'd known it might only be a small aircraft with little room for a heavy and bulky suitcase.

Gideon saw to the small airport formalities and she followed him out to a waiting car. The cold no longer bothered her. It was late, dark and her nerves were stretched. She got into the car with no idea where they were going—she just wanted to find Justine.

Kit's brother was highly efficient, she discovered, for after they had been driving some while the driver pulled up outside a smart hotel. It was not the same one that had been pictured on Justine's postcard.

The driver got out and opened the door for her. She found herself standing beside Gideon Langford while he relieved the driver of their small amount of luggage.

'What are we doing?' she asked, her wits seeming to be numb.

'I've booked a couple of rooms here,' he replied. He had taken care of her accommodation too, apparently, and he was already turning to go into the hotel.

'I want to go to…' She wanted to say Justine's name, but was caught out by an emotional moment and could not. 'The other hotel.'

'So do I—we'll check in first,' he decreed, and Ellena realised, as she followed him into the smart hotel and he summoned someone in authority, that Gideon Langford, once he'd had an update on the situation, had always intended to go and check out the other hotel whether she went with him or not.

Ellena stood by him aware that he, or someone in his employ, must have phoned ahead so they'd have somewhere to stay. The local police had been informed that their plane had arrived, apparently, and they, with the hotel manager, adjourned to a private room—but only to hear that there were no new developments, that everything was as bleak as had been forecast. A well-rehearsed plan had been put into operation, with rescue teams combing the area—they had reported back that there was absolutely no chance of anyone caught in that avalanche surviving.

Ellena strove valiantly for control. She could not believe it, would not believe it. Nor, apparently, would Gideon Langford. Stiffly he thanked everyone for their efforts and, flicking a glance to where Ellena stood dry-eyed and taut with control, said, 'And now, Miss Spencer and I would like to see where our relatives were staying.'

She hated that word 'were', the past tense, even if logic said loudly and clearly that since

Justine and Kit were not around to occupy their hotel accommodation, 'were' very clearly fitted.

They left their luggage to be taken up to their rooms, and drove away from their hotel in the same car in which they had arrived. This time, though, with a police escort. The reason was explained—and also why they were booked into a different hotel—when they got to the place where Kit and Justine had been staying. Regardless of the lateness of the hour and the risk of frostbite, some of the press, having been blocked at the small airport, were keen to have an interview with the missing man's brother.

Ellena had been aware that Gideon Langford was well known. How well known was borne out by the fact that he knew some of the newsmen by their first names. 'You know as much as I do, John,' he answered one reporter, while at the same time ushering Ellena inside the hotel.

'Who's the lady?' someone else asked—they did not get a reply.

The hotel manager showed them up to the room which Kit and Justine had used. 'I have not had the room disturbed,' the Austrian assured them, and, receiving their polite thanks, sensitively went out, closing the door behind him.

Only then, alone with Gideon Langford, did it dawn on Ellena, having been in his company for some hours now, how little conversation had passed between them.

Nor did she feel like talking then. She stared round the twin-bedded compact room, imagined she could hear Justine and Kit's laughter, the way they had been laughing that last Saturday—abruptly she blanked her mind off, and became aware of Gideon Langford opening drawers and poking about in wardrobes.

'There are a few clothes here—but no suitcases,' he stated matter-of-factly.

Ellena went over to the open wardrobe and, standing next to him, observed a couple of ancient anoraks which she recognised as belonging to Kit and Justine.

'M-my sister was going to buy new,' she informed him chokily. 'She was—is—oh, dammit...' Her voice broke; she turned from him, determined to gain control. Justine wasn't dead, she wasn't, and she wasn't going to cry. 'Justine is going to buy a whole new wardrobe,' she made herself continue.

She guessed Gideon was having a hard time with his emotions as well, when he retorted shortly, 'Kit didn't have any money!'

Even so, that annoyed her. It gave her the stiffening she needed, anyhow, as she retorted straight back: 'Then perhaps it's just as well Justine had her own money—she probably paid for this trip.' Immediately the acid words were out she felt contrite. She flicked a glance at him, saw he didn't seem to view her as his favourite person, and at once she apologised, 'I'm sorry, Mr Langford, I'm trying so hard not to go to pieces. I d-didn't mean to give you the rough end of it.'

Whether he accepted her apology she had no idea, for he just stood and stared at her from those steady slate-grey eyes. But she rather guessed she had been forgiven when, turning from her, he grunted, 'Gideon.'

She felt she should curtsy, then wondered if stress had made her light-headed. But she forgot everything save Justine when she spied in one of the open drawers a sweater she had lent her one time.

'No, definitely no suitcases,' Gideon announced, sounding positive.

'If you're thinking that they may have packed up and left—and you can't wish it any more than I—I have to tell you, Justine in the main is so happy-go-lucky. She planned to buy anything she needed here—she's just as likely to have arrived without luggage.'

'Or followed Kit's example and packed anything she might have thought of in a plastic carrier,' he documented, adding, 'As you remarked, a pair well met.'

They stayed another few minutes in the room but there were no more clues to be picked up; only a few toiletries were left in the bathroom. Ellena could feel her emotions on the brink of spilling over, and had not Gideon suggested they leave she would have made the suggestion herself.

They had chance of a private word with the hotelier, who promised he would contact them instantly, should his guests return. Then, again running the gauntlet of a couple of hardy pressmen, they returned to their own hotel.

Gideon Langford had a room opposite hers and, having escorted her up in the lift, he went into her room with her. 'Will you be all right here?' he enquired courteously.

'Yes, thank you,' she replied politely.

He didn't leave straight away, but stayed to suggest, 'You'll want to phone your parents.'

'My parents are dead,' she answered tonelessly.

'You're on your own?'

Ross
Rita K

HOLD SLIP

User name: Ross, Rita K
Phone number: 330-476-6029
Pickup By: 10/12/2022
Item ID: 32487004898335
Title: Married in a moment [large print]

_____

_____ LM /w/ Patron
_____ LM /w/ Machine
_____ LM /w/
_____ Not Working #
_____ Voicemail Full
_____ No Answer
Other: _____

Date: _____ Initial: _____
_____

HELD FOR 7 DAYS!

CHECKOUT SLIP
Carroll County Bookmobile
Date charged: 9/19/2022,8:46
Title: With his ring [large print]
Item ID: 32771000794030

Due: 10/17/2022
****

Date charged: 9/19/2022,8:46
Title: To stay forever [large print]
Item ID: 32771000299162

Due: 10/17/2022
****

Date charged: 9/19/2022,8:46
Title: A wife in waiting [large print]
Item ID: 32771000756013

Due: 10/17/2022
****

Date charged: 9/19/2022,8:46
Title: Married in a moment [large print]
Item ID: 32487004898335

Due: 10/17/2022
****

www.carrolllibrary.org

'No,' she denied. No way was she ready to accept that Justine wasn't coming back.

'You live with someone?' he asked sharply, and she just knew he meant some man.

'I live alone,' she responded curtly.

'Goodnight!' Gideon Langford turned away from her, obviously fed up.

'I'm sorry,' she found herself apologising. 'I'm—on edge.'

He halted at the door and turned round, relenting, 'We both are.' And then proceeded to instruct, 'Try and get some rest. Have anything you need brought to your room. With a few pressmen around, you'd better stay where you are until I come for you.' He made to leave, thought for a moment, and then said, 'I may be out some time tomorrow. I'll contact you as soon as I get back.'

'Where are you going?'

He hesitated, but then did her the courtesy of being honest with her. 'Out to the avalanche site.'

'I'm coming with you,' she said at once, no please or thank you.

'I don't think—'

'I'm coming!' she butted in. If he thought she was going to stay here while he went there—

where Justine and Kit might be—he could think again!

He shrugged, 'Suit yourself,' and left her.

Ellena supposed she must have slept at some time—it didn't feel like it. She was up at six, showered and dressed and waiting for Gideon Langford's call.

It wasn't long in coming. He would see her in half an hour's time. Meanwhile, he had some breakfast sent up to her room. Ellena wasn't hungry, but drank some strong hot coffee and belatedly remembered work she was supposed to be doing that day.

She put through a call to Andrea in England and explained why, and where she was. 'I'm not sure when I'll be back,' she warned.

'Don't worry about it,' Andrea answered warmly. 'Take as long as you need, Ellena,' she suggested gently. 'We'll all be hoping for you.'

Gideon Langford, when he knocked on her door, was not in talkative mood. 'There's no news?' she asked urgently.

He shook his head. 'Ready?'

Wordlessly she went with him out of the hotel and to the waiting car, and said not another word in the hour-long drive to where the disaster had occurred.

There were some officials waiting for them, but when, after walking some way, they stood back and pointed and explained about the mass of snow, and the boulders and rocks it had brought down in its wake, Ellena could see for herself that anyone foolhardy enough to chance ski-ing in that area would not have stood a chance.

She felt what little colour she had in her face drain away, felt gut-wrenching pain and wanted to scream, and to go on screaming. She turned away, collided into someone. It was Gideon. His arms came around her. He held her. They held each other, two human beings in need of solace. She guessed that, like her, he had always looked out for his younger sibling and it had been a role taken on willingly. She wanted the holding to go on.

Ellena broke from him, her mind in a turmoil. Somehow she got back to the car; somehow Gideon was there too. The car was moving, she staring unseeing out of one window on one side, he staring unseeing out of the window on the other side.

They had been driving on the return journey for some while. Ellena was still feeling stunned, shaken, and still not ready to believe it, to believe that she had lost her sister, that poor little

Violette had lost her parents, when suddenly it hit her that the poor little scrap might have been orphaned.

'Oh, no!' escaped her on an anguished cry of sound, and as Gideon Langford turned from his non-contemplation of the view, she whispered, 'What about the baby!'

'Baby?' he echoed, and sounded so startled that Ellena came to, realising she was not alone. 'What baby?' he questioned tautly.

She moved from her own non-contemplation of the view to look at him. And it was her turn to be startled. For clearly Gideon Langford had no idea that Kit had a baby daughter. A daughter of four months old.

Astonished, she realised that Gideon Langford had no idea at all that he was an uncle!

CHAPTER TWO

'YOU didn't know?' Ellena gasped.

'Baby?' he clipped, clearly wanting to know more, and quickly.

There was no way to dress it up, nor, a shock though it might be to him, try to hide it. 'Justine and Kit have a four-month-old daughter,' she replied, and saw a muscle jerk in his strong, good-looking face. Saw him take what she had said on board—and realised that a dozen and one pertinent questions were on their way. But then she saw him flick a glance at their driver, who understood a little English—and Gideon turned from her to renew his non-contemplation of the view from the vehicle's side window. He had obviously swallowed down those questions but Ellena did not doubt that she would be on the receiving end of them the moment there were no other ears around to overhear what they were saying. Gideon Langford was well known but, indisputably, he valued his family privacy—and there were pressmen about.

A cold, stiff silence stretched between them and lasted until they arrived at their hotel.

Gideon Langford asked for the keys to their rooms. He hung onto them as they went up in the lift and inserted the key into the door of her room. He pushed the door open. She preceded him into her room, knowing that he would follow.

Ellena went over to the window, again looking out but registering nothing very much. She heard the sound of the door behind her being closed. She turned. She was not mistaken, she saw: Gideon Langford had not merely opened the door and left her to it, he was right there with her. Those questions weren't going to wait any longer—he wanted answers.

Why she should feel hostile to his questioning she had no idea, a self-defence mechanism perhaps? But when he began, 'This child...' for short, pithy starters, she discovered an aggressiveness in her that rushed out to meet anything he had to say head-on.

'Kit and Justine's baby, you mean?' she challenged before he could get further.

Her aggressiveness glanced off him, barely touching him, though she didn't miss the way his eyes narrowed slightly at her tone. 'You're saying my brother is the father of your sister's child?'

'Of course he is!' she erupted.

'You're sure of it?'

How dared he? 'Listen, you,' she attacked hotly, 'Justine may have been a bit wild, a bit of a rebel, and their relationship may have had its—its stormy moments, but there's been no other man for her but Kit, since the moment she met and fell in love with him!'

'But they're not married?'

'Grief—he's your brother—don't you know anything about him?'

'I know a whole lot about him, including the fact that there was no woman on the scene when I last visited him six months ago.'

'Your bi-annual visit, was it?' she threw in tartly, though she almost apologised for that remark when he flicked her an acid look. Then she wondered why the hell should she? Who did he think he was, trying to deny Kit was the baby's father? 'Justine lived at home with me until the baby was born—Kit collected them from the hospital and there didn't seem to be any question that he would take them back to his flat.'

'They live together?'

'Happily,' Ellena declared frostily.

'Happily unmarried?'

'I don't think getting married occurred to either of them,' she replied honestly.

'That sounds like Kit,' Gideon muttered, and asked abruptly, 'Where is it now—this infant?'

She felt annoyed. 'Violette,' she informed him stiffly. 'Her name's Violette.'

'Violette?' he echoed—much in the same vein as if she'd told him they'd called the child Rover.

'They chose the name, not me!' she snapped, and wondered if the stress was getting more than she could take, because her sense of humour seemed to be twitching for a smiling release at his reaction to the baby's name. She did not smile, however, but informed him, 'Your brother Russell and his wife are looking after Violette while—'

'Your sister left a four-month-old baby with that hard-nosed, money-grubbing bitch!' he interrupted on a snarl.

Ellena blinked in surprise—all too evidently Gideon Langford had little time for his sister-in-law. She recalled that Justine had called Pamela a bit of a shrew; the one and only time she had spoken with her herself, she hadn't taken to her, either.

'Your brother left the baby too!' she defended. 'Anyway, as well as paying Pamela, Justine also engaged a temporary nanny.'

'Huh!' he grunted, and Ellena started to actively dislike him. 'I phoned Russell just before I left—he didn't say anything about looking after Kit's infant!'

'That's hardly my fault!' she flew, her emotions all over the place, her temper seeming to be on a very short fuse. 'Since you're a family who only visit every six months, it's a wonder to me you tell each other anything.'

The chill factor went down another ten degrees as Gideon Langford favoured her with an icy look for her trouble. 'You know nothing!' he rapped curtly.

'I know...' she went to explode. But then was suddenly so overcome by the events that had taken place that she came to a full stop, words failing her. She swallowed hard, emotion threatening to overwhelm her.

She turned swiftly about, her grief private, not to be shared. She looked down at the windowsill, concentrated hard on it, striving with all she had for control.

So hard was she battling not to break down that she momentarily forgot she wasn't alone in the room. A reminder of Gideon Langford's presence arrived, though, when, just as if he knew of her every thought and feeling, he moved behind her and took hold of her.

She felt his firm grip on her upper arms and began to like him again, even though all the evidence pointed to the reverse. 'Hang on, Ellena,' he instructed low in her right ear, using her first name, making them more friends than the enemies they'd been a minute ago. 'They're not dead. I won't believe they're dead.'

She swallowed hard, but did not turn around. 'I can't believe it either,' she said huskily.

For a minute more Gideon held her in that steadying grip. Then he was saying, 'We have to think of leaving.'

'I don't want to leave—I can't,' she answered.

'Yes, you can,' he countered. 'I'll instruct everyone you can think of to contact me the moment they have the barest hint of news.'

She tried to be sensible. 'You've business to get back to, I expect.'

'It seems incidental,' he replied—and Ellena knew that she really did like him. He had a multi-million pound conglomerate to run, but it meant nothing to him when his youngest brother was missing.

She realised, common sense giving her a nudge, that they could achieve nothing by staying. 'When do you want to leave?' she asked, and felt him give her arms a small squeeze of encouragement.

'As soon as you're ready,' he answered, letting go his hold and moving away.

Ellena turned and looked at him. The icy look he had served her with before had gone, and, for all he was unsmiling, he seemed less harsh than he had been. 'I'll just get my things together, settle up here, and...'

'I'll settle,' he stated, and, when she looked likely to proudly protest, 'You're family,' he said, and went, not knowing how warmed she felt. For, apart from Justine and Violette, she had no other family.

It took her next to no time to gather her belongings together. But in that short period Gideon Langford had settled their account with the hotel and organised their flight.

They were on their way back to the small airport when she realised he'd found time to speak with other people too. 'The minister from the local church was kind enough to call,' he informed her quietly as they reached their destination. 'He wondered if we would like him to carry out a service for Kit and Justine.'

'You thanked him, but said no I hope,' she answered jerkily.

She realised that she and Gideon Langford must be pretty well near on the same wave-length when he replied, 'I did. It sounded too final.' He, by the sound of it, was not ready to admit to that finality yet—and neither was she.

In contrast to the silence that had existed between them on the journey out, they had been in the air around ten minutes when Gideon Langford looked across the small aisle at her and enquired, 'You mentioned your sister has money of her own; does that mean that neither of you has to work?'

'Justine never did get the hang of working,' Ellena replied truthfully. 'Though the way she's spending, she'll be lucky if her money lasts her longer than a couple of years.'

'It was an inheritance?'

'Money our parents invested for both of us to have when we reached twenty.'

'You're—how old?'

Ellena stared at him from frank blue eyes. Nothing like asking! He'd be demanding how much the investment was next. 'Twenty-two,' she answered. 'I received my money two years ago.'

'But you've still some of it left?'

Was there a purpose behind his questioning—it escaped her if there was. 'Some of it

went—cars for Justine and me, clothes, and...
But, yes, there's still a little left,' she owned.

'From your remarks about your sister not getting the hang of working—and that's not a crit-
icism,' he slipped in, causing her to realise she
must have bridled a touch without knowing it,
'Kit is very much the same,' he soothed any
ruffled feathers. 'But, to get back, I take it that
you *do* know the meaning of the word
"work"?'

'I enjoy my job so much I hardly think of it
as work,' she owned.

'What sort of work would that be?'

He had a certain kind of charm, she realised.
Sufficient, anyway, to have her put her present
worries to the back of her mind for a short
while. 'I'm an accountant,' she answered, and,
because that sounded a little like showing off,
'Though I've only recently qualified.'

'Who are you with?' he wanted to know.

'A. Keyte and Company,' she replied, and,
realising it was a very small business compared
with the enormous accountancy firm he must
deal with, she added, 'It's only a tiny company,
but I love it there.' Agonising thoughts and worries were soon back as she relayed, 'I rang
Andrea this morning. She said to take as much
time as I...' Her voice tapered off. Ellena

looked away from him as she fought for and gained control of her emotions. 'Anyhow, much as I enjoy working for her, I may have to look elsewhere.'

'You have some problem?'

She glanced across at him again. He had seemed so much on her wavelength about almost everything, it surprised her that he wasn't this time. 'Well, I'll obviously try to make some arrangements that will mean I don't have to leave my present employer, but if all else fails, I shall have to try and find a firm that has crèche facilities. V—'

'You're thinking of taking that baby to live with you?' He seemed astounded at the very idea!

But that he should be astounded at something which, to her mind, was a foregone conclusion, annoyed her. 'Naturally, I'm taking her,' she stated forcefully. Adding, for good measure, '*That* baby is my niece!'

Only to be left staring at him open-mouthed when, 'And mine!' he stated quietly, purposefully.

Ellena closed her mouth, but was still staring at him incredulously, still not believing the deliberate intent behind his quietly spoken words. She just could not take in that he seemed to be saying that he wanted charge of Violette. Then her feeling of shock gave way to a feeling of fury—fury born of panic. Over her dead body! 'You can't possibly want her!' she erupted furiously. 'You've had nothing to do with her. I've seen her most every weekend!' she staked her claim. 'In the week, too, if her parents needed a babysitter,' she tacked on for extra strength. 'Why,' she hurried on, barely pausing for breath, 'you didn't even know of Violette's existence until I told you about—'

'So now I do know,' he cut in calmly. 'And I have as much right as you to...'

'No, you haven't!' she denied. 'You don't know her, you don't love her, you...'

'You live in a *flat* near Croydon.' When had she told him that? She was too het up to remember. 'I have a house in open country.'

Who said her flat wasn't in open country? It was a wasted argument, she realised. 'You led me on!' she accused him furiously.

'How the devil did I do that?' he challenged harshly.

'You know!' she hurled back. 'Finding out that while I have some funds they're peanuts in relation to your wealth. Finding out that I have to work, so I won't be able to be with Violette all the time. You're despicable! You're...'

'You're off your head!' he countered. 'It hadn't so much as occurred to me that you'd want guardianship of that infant when I indulged in a little—polite conversation—to help the flight along.'

'Polite conversation, my aunt Fanny!' she tossed at him rudely, not believing it for a minute. 'Well, you may make a claim for her, *Mr* Langford, but I'm having her!' No way was she going to let the poor mite live with this brute!

'I'll see you in court,' he drawled—and that infuriated her. Just because he had more money, a house in the country, he thought he could ride roughshod over other people. She loved the baby but he didn't even know her!

'You won't stand a chance!' Surely love came before money?

'How do you figure that?'

She hadn't yet. But, thus challenged, she slammed at him, 'I've an unsullied reputation, for one thing!'

His look said, How boring. 'You mean with the opposite sex?' he drawled, and she wished she'd kept her mouth closed. But that How boring expression niggled her, forcing her on.

'Which is more than can be said for you!' she attacked sniffily.

'It's true, I've had my moments,' he admitted mockingly. 'But are you saying that you've *never* had any member of the opposite sex— er—staying over?'

'That's got nothing to do with you!' she retorted hotly, starting to feel a shade warm around the ears.

'It has, if you intend to stand up in court and swear to it,' he derided.

He was infuriating. True, her experience of men was limited, though she was certain that there couldn't be many around like him! 'I'm prepared to do that if I have to,' she told him snappily.

'Ye gods!' he exclaimed, seeming to find it incredible that she'd reached twenty-two without being tempted.

And that annoyed her. 'From what I hear, you were chief practitioner of the love 'em and leave 'em ethic.'

He shrugged. 'Charm has its own reward,' he owned modestly. But, apparently done with ribbing her, 'Straight up—are you a virgin?' he wanted to know.

It wasn't just her ears that felt warm. She was certain her cheeks positively glowed. 'It's nothing to be ashamed of!' she snapped.

'Did I say it was?'

He hadn't. But she didn't want this conversation, though she wasn't sure if it hadn't been her who had started it. 'We're getting away from the point,' she said heatedly.

'Which is?'

Give her strength! 'The point is, you, with your lifestyle. Well, you're hardly the type to be responsible for the upbringing of a young girl, are you?'

'If she's only four months old, I'd guess she isn't even walking yet!'

'She'll grow!' Ellena retorted, glaring at him, feeling panickily that she was somehow getting the worst of this.

She was positive of it when, having tired of the argument, it seemed, he decreed, 'Perhaps we'll leave it for some judge to decide.'

Ellena did not answer. Suddenly it dawned on her that she and Gideon were talking as if Justine and Kit weren't coming back—and they were. *They were!* Whether the same thought had just struck Gideon she couldn't have said, but she thought she caught a glimpse of a bleak look come to his expression a moment before he turned his head away.

Ellena turned her face to her window too. Conversation between them, polite or otherwise, was done with, and she spent the rest of the flight on trying to keep thoughts that Justine might be dead out of her mind. Instead she endeavoured to concentrate on what must be done to ensure that Violette had a safe, warm and loving upbringing.

From the sound of it, Gideon Langford was fully prepared to go to court to battle for custody of the baby. With his money, he was going to be able to afford to employ the very best of lawyers.

What she must do, she realised, was to get herself in a position to combat everything he threw at her. Had a house in the country, did he? Well, albeit that hers would probably be pokey by comparison, she'd get a house in the country too.

She'd probably got enough money left to put down a deposit on something small. And she was earning more now, so a mortgage of not too vast proportions was within her means. She'd got enough furniture to furnish somewhere modest and—and…

Her thoughts fractured and her mind hurried on to taking the baby's cot and all necessities from Kit's flat. She gained control and decided she would only *borrow* them for the short term, until Kit and Justine came for Violette.

Ellena fought another battle for control—and managed to win. She was making all these plans unnecessarily. Justine and Kit would be back soon. As likely as they were to take themselves off ski-ing in a prohibited area, they were equally as likely—leaving bits and pieces of clothing behind—to up sticks and move on somewhere else, if the mood took them. The very worrying thing about that, though, was that whatever else Justine was or was not, she was scrupulously honest. No way would she dream of doing a flit without paying her hotel bill, Ellena just knew it. It just wasn't in her sister's make-up—and yet, that hotel bill had not been paid.

Telling herself that everybody was allowed one lapse, and that, what with having just had a baby and everything, Justine's hormones were probably still all over the place—sufficiently, anyhow, for her to act in a way she wouldn't normally—Ellena suddenly had one very bright positive thought, that was startling in its simplicity.

Possession, it was said, was nine-tenths of the law. So what was to stop her from going to Russell and Pamela Langford's home and taking possession of Violette? To hear Justine tell it, and Gideon Langford too, for that matter, Pamela Langford was only interested in money.

No problem. If Justine had not settled with her and the temporary nanny in advance, then she could easily do so. Did she have any proof with her that she was who she said she was? Of course, she had her passport with her. And both Pamela and Russell Langford, from the two times she had telephoned, would know the name Ellena Spencer. Though, come to think of it, she would have to call at her flat first to pick up Russell Langford's address and her car.

The plane started to descend. Ellena couldn't wait to be on her way. Andrea had said, 'Take as much time as you need...' There was a lot to do. First things first, though; she was making tracks for Hertfordshire...

Gideon Langford's organisation was highly efficient, she discovered, after they had landed. Someone—the pilot or whoever—must have notified someone of their estimated time of arrival. In any event, there were two chauffeur-driven cars waiting for them.

'George will drive you to your home,' Gideon Langford explained, plainly heading in another direction himself, no doubt to some high-powered business meeting.

'Thank you,' she answered politely.

'I'll be in touch.'

You mean your lawyers will! But civility cost nothing and, even if Gideon had sprouted horns, give the devil his due, thus far she had reason to be grateful to him. She extended a hand. 'Thank you for everything,' she said sincerely.

They shook hands. 'Goodbye,' he said.

She turned away. She had urgent business to attend to. She doubted the next time she saw him—in court—that they would be so civil with each other.

In the limousine she gave thought to what must be done. She didn't want this fight, this tug of war. Please God, Justine and Kit would be back before the fight got started.

She vaguely remembered something in the newspapers only recently, about a magistrate or judge sitting in emergency session of the family division of the court when someone needed an instant decision on what was best for a child. Ellena had only her own love-filled childhood to go on. But surely it was better for a child to be brought up where love was?

Worriedly, she instinctively knew where love *was not*, and that was with Pamela and Russell Langford. It was possible that in future—if he could spare time away from his other non-work activities—that Gideon might get to know and love his niece. Though she doubted he would see much of her. It went without saying that he would hire a nanny... All this wasn't going to happen, though. Bearing in mind that Violette's parents would come home—she must believe that; *she must*—Ellena sincerely felt she would be letting Justine down if she allowed anyone to have guardianship of the baby but herself.

At her flat Ellena thanked George very much. 'It's not heavy,' she smiled when it seemed he would carry her bag indoors for her.

Once she was in her flat, Ellena raced around finding the address she needed, and was again on her way. She could, she realised, have left Violette with Pamela and Russell Langford for the duration Justine had contracted with them. But fear that Gideon Langford would take pre-emptive action spurred her on. Should it come to a court hearing, she wanted it established that Violette—a healthy, happy Violette—lived with her.

Ellena stopped briefly on her way to buy a baby car seat and a few other essential purchases for Violette, and was soon speeding on again. She did wonder if she should ring the Langfords to let them know she was coming. She decided against it. Gideon might ring Russell at any time to tell him the latest con-

cerning Austria. She didn't want Russell revealing that she'd phoned. She didn't want
Gideon knowing anything until after her visit.

She arrived at the address she was seeking, a
very smart house in its own grounds, with hope
in her heart that her own neighbours would bear
with her when she brought a baby home to her
flat. There was a very sleek and expensive car
on the drive of the Langfords' home which
hinted that, for all they were accepting payment
for looking after Russell's niece, they weren't
too badly off.

Ellena rang the doorbell, with her thoughts on
the early possibility of maybe renting somewhere where children were allowed; only on a
short lease while she got somewhere more permanent arranged.

The door was opened almost at once.
'Good...' she began as part of her greeting, but
the rest didn't get said. The sleek and expensive
car didn't belong to Russell Langford, she
swiftly realised. It belonged to his brother,
Gideon! Gideon Langford, having changed the
chauffeur-driven vehicle for his own car, had
got there before her!

'Traffic's a nightmare at this time of day, isn't
it?' he murmured blandly.

It wasn't funny! The fact that he had beaten her to it wasn't funny at all so why did she find his remark amusing? Not that she'd let him see, of course.

'What are you doing here?' she demanded.

He looked ready to put her in her place for trying to demand anything. But, to her surprise, instead he clipped out the words, 'Just leaving!'

He was still there, though, when a man, not so tall as Gideon by a couple of inches, and fair haired, with the same features as Kit, came along the hall with a sharp-looking auburn-haired woman in tow. The woman looked hostile before they even started. 'Yes?' she challenged irritably.

Ellena opened her mouth but, to her surprise, heard Gideon Langford say pleasantly, 'Ellena, I don't think you know my brother, Russell, and his wife, do you?' Smoothly, he introduced them, and, while Ellena was seriously wishing that he would just clear off, he stayed to hear her business.

Russell Langford invited her into the sitting room—of the baby and her temporary nanny there was no sign. Gideon returned to the sitting room with them. Ellena tossed him an Afraid-of-missing-something? kind of look. He smiled back, though it was an insincere smile.

'G-Gideon will have told you the news concerning Austria,' she began.

'Bad do,' Russell replied, the way he had when she had telephoned him. Was it only last night? It seemed weeks ago!

'The thing is that while I c-can't believe...' she took a shaky breath '...that we'll never see Justine and Kit again,' she gained control to continue, 'I feel, with your permission, of course, that they would want me to look after Violette until they get back.'

'Now isn't that strange? That's more or less exactly what Gideon said!' Pamela Langford answered for her husband waspishly.

Ellena guessed she should have expected, from what he'd said on the plane, that Gideon would not drag his heels in taking some action. What was unexpected, though, was that Pamela Langford would look at her with such blatant hostility. Then it was that Ellena recalled Gideon saying something about Pamela being a money-grubbing bitch, and, although she was wishing that Gideon would just get to his car and go, there seemed nothing for it but to conduct her business in front of him.

'I'm sorry,' she apologised as pleasantly as she was able. 'I know there are some—er—money matters outstanding.' She knew nothing of the sort, but realised that if Justine hadn't paid Pamela in advance, then outstanding the matter of money must be. 'Naturally I'll settle what Justine owes y—'

'That child was left in our charge!' Pamela Langford cut in loudly, coldly. 'And in our charge is where she'll stay!'

Oh, heavens! Ellena felt tremendously taken aback. She hadn't expected this sort of reception! 'I appreciate that you want to do what's right,' she began, forcing herself to be placatory—she had not the smallest intention of leaving her niece with this cold, unfeeling woman. 'But...'

'But nothing. The child stays here,' Pamela Langford cut in sourly. Ellena looked from her to Russell—he was looking anywhere but at her or his brother—no use appealing to him! Not that she wanted to set husband and wife against each other. And, given he wanted the same as she wanted, she couldn't expect any help from Gideon. Which was just as well, because, while silently absorbing everything that was taking place, Gideon Langford was not offering her any help. 'I'll show you out,' Pamela stated frostily.

'I'd like to see Violette if I may.' Ellena refused to budge.

'She's upstairs asleep. I'm not going to have her disturbed again; it will take hours for her nanny to shut her up.'

Ellena was aware that Violette's needs were nothing in this alien household, and felt a desperate need to check that the little mite was being properly cared for. 'I won't disturb her,' she stated, still refusing to budge.

'That's right, you won't,' Pamela Langford answered nastily.

Ellena felt frustrated beyond bearing by the woman's attitude. She couldn't leave without seeing the baby, she couldn't. Then, just as she was about to insist that she must see her, Gideon Langford chipped in, to tell her quietly, 'I've seen the baby, Ellena; she seems well looked after and healthy.'

Ellena turned to him swiftly, not knowing why she trusted him when she didn't feel she could trust his sister-in-law. 'She's all right?' she asked urgently. 'She looks happy?'

He gave her a slightly sardonic smile as though to say, What do I know about four-month-old babies? 'She wasn't crying,' he said.

Ellena turned back to Pamela Langford. 'Perhaps you'd tell me when it would be convenient for me to spend some time with my niece.'

'We'll arrange visiting rights through the courts,' was the vinegary reply—and as the import of those words took root, Ellena didn't trust herself to answer.

She went to the door. Pamela Langford, as though she didn't trust her not to dart up the stairs, went with her. Ellena was forced to accept then that she was not going to see Violette that day, and took what solace she could from the fact that Gideon had seen the baby and, albeit that his knowledge of infants was limited, he thought she seemed well looked after and healthy.

She half expected him to follow her out. After all he had been about to leave when she'd arrived. But he was obviously staying behind to have a word more with his brother.

Ellena drove home in a very upset frame of mind. Over the last few hours she had received one shock after another. Last night she had learned that Justine and Kit were missing; earlier today she had learned that Gideon was prepared to go to court over the guardianship of their child. And now, here was Pamela Langford—a woman she had found it impossible to warm to—talking of court action! What chance, Ellena wondered, did she have of loving and nurturing Violette until Justine and Kit came home?

After another fretful night, Ellena awoke on Friday morning with the same thoughts going around in her head. She was in two minds about going to her office. But realising that, if she didn't change her job—and her plans of yesterday seemed to be getting further and further away from her—she was going to need time off work for court appearances; no way was she going to give up Violette without a fight. Ellena decided she had better go to work.

'We didn't expect to see you!' Andrea Keyte exclaimed when she walked in.

'I may need time off later,' Ellena replied without thinking.

'Want to talk about it?'

Andrea had been a wonderful friend and very forbearing with regard to previous crises Ellena had had over Justine. And normally Ellena might have confided in her this time. Only now, depending how things went, there was a possibility that in the interest of Violette's daycare, she might have to resign. Andrea had enough to worry about running her business, without Ellena giving out hints at this early stage that she might, or might not, be leaving.

'Thanks, but not just now.'

Ellena went to her own office, suddenly realising that if she hired a nanny herself, that would solve the problem of Violette's daycare. She wouldn't have to leave. She took out some work, though her thoughts became desperate that she might not need a nanny if Pamela Langford or her brother-in-law, Gideon, were granted guardianship, and her concentration wasn't all it should be. What she needed, Ellena realised, was some legal advice.

She was just contemplating ringing the solicitor who had always handled her parents' affairs, and who had handled the legalities of selling their house for her and Justine, when the protector of the firm's switchboard rang.

'I've a man named Langford on the phone for you, are you available?' Lucy asked.

Langford? Which one? With hope in her heart that it was Russell, calling to tell her that he and his wife were prepared to let the baby go, she requested, 'Put him through, Lucy,' hearing the click as she did so. 'Russell?' Ellena asked.

'Gideon,' came the reply—and her thoughts went racing in another direction.

'You've heard something—from Austria?' she questioned urgently, half in fear of bad news, half in hope of good news.

'Afraid not,' he answered instantly.

'Oh,' she said dully. But he hadn't taken time out of his day merely to chat. 'What can I do for you?' she asked, knowing in advance that she wasn't going to lift a finger to help if he was still insistent on claiming guardianship of Violette.

'I'd like to see you,' he stated.

Why her heart should give a little flip just then, she had no idea. He wasn't asking her for a date, for goodness' sake! Not that she'd go out with him if he was. 'I've a full appointments book today.' She countered that peculiar little heartbeat—why should she want to see him? Grief!

'I meant outside of business hours. I'd like to call round at your flat this evening. Unless, of course, you'd prefer we shared dinner while we…'

'My flat will be fine,' she said hurriedly, too late realising that in her haste to show him she had no wish to have dinner with him, she had taken another option she didn't want either. 'Presumably this is in connection with the baby?' she queried, just to let him know that she wasn't interested in entertaining him socially.

'Of course,' he replied, just as if the notion of seeing her socially had never for a minuscule moment so much as occurred to him. 'Seven-thirty?'

'Seven-thirty,' she agreed. Simultaneously their phones went down.

Ellena seemed to take a queue of phone calls after that, some of them needing action, so it was lunchtime by the time she got round to ringing her solicitor. 'Mr Ollerenshaw has left for the day on other business,' his secretary informed her. 'He'll be out of the office until Monday—can anyone else help?'

Ellena declined, but made an appointment to see Mr Ollerenshaw on Monday. She liked the fatherly man and, as well as having a first-class legal head on his shoulders, she remembered him as being warm and kind. She'd wait and see what Gideon Langford had to say that evening, and perhaps would have more to check with Mr Ollerenshaw on Monday.

She was late getting home. That wasn't unusual on a Friday. She liked to clear her desk, and, having had Thursday off work, there had been yesterday's work to catch up on. She just had time to make herself a sandwich and ponder on whether she should make Gideon one too. She raised her eyes skywards—was she going mad? This man was coming to try and talk her into forfeiting any claim she intended to make for Violette. If he hadn't had dinner—let him starve!

Ellena did consider changing from her smart all-wool light navy suit and into trousers and shirt. She decided against it. She had an idea that to take away her business suit for something less formal might give him the edge, make her oddly vulnerable somehow. Oh, rot, she was letting her fear that the Langford family would take Violette from her get to her.

Gideon Langford arrived a minute after the appointed time. 'You found the address all right, then,' she commented. He was in her home and good manners decreed she was polite to him to start with—even if he'd be leaving with a flea in his ear! 'Coffee?' she enquired, her good manners working overtime. She had never thought her sitting room tiny, but he seemed to fill it.

'Thanks,' he accepted, and wandered out to her kitchen and watched her while she made the coffee.

In her view, depending on what he had to say, he might not be around long enough to drink it, but—painful though it was to remember—he need not have offered her a lift to Austria in his private jet on Wednesday.

She made herself a coffee as well and carried a tray to the sitting room. 'Take a seat,' she invited and, sitting down herself, looked at him opposite her, his long legs stretched out some way. 'Have you seen Violette today?' she asked by way of an opening as he drank some of his coffee.

'No,' he replied, and asked sharply, 'Have you?'

She shook her head, and saw no harm in revealing, 'I'm taking legal advice on Monday.'

'An excellent idea,' Gideon answered to her surprise. 'Though I may be able to save you the trouble.'

'I don't think...' she began stiffly—bubbles to him and his saving her anything! He was a Langford—in this instance, he was the enemy!

'I took legal advice myself last night, as a matter of fact,' he cut in, stunning her somewhat.

'Well, don't let the grass grow!' she retorted crossly.

'Now, don't get angry,' Gideon said calmly. 'Russell I can handle, but if you knew his wife better than you do, you'd know to have your ammunition ready to spike her guns and get in there first.'

By the sound of it, Gideon Langford was going to fight his sister-in-law with everything he had. And while one meeting with Pamela Langford was sufficient for Ellena to know she would fight with everything at her disposal too, to ensure that Violette was brought up in a far more loving home, she was also aware that that meant opposing Gideon.

Ellena swallowed down her crossness. Gideon had finished his coffee, and they hadn't really begun their discussion yet in earnest. 'You don't sound as if you like your sister-in-law very much,' she commented.

'I don't,' he stated bluntly. 'Among other things, she's taken over the ruination of my brother from his mother, and…'

'Oh!' Ellena exclaimed, startled. 'Your mother—um—spoilt him?'

'Like you'd never believe! Well-intentioned though she was, she had an unshakeable belief that the middle child in any family was grievously disadvantaged. I'm afraid she overcompensated to extremes.'

Ellena stared at him, fascinated by this insight into his family. Somehow she knew that wild horses would not normally have dragged this information from Gideon. So, without knowing quite how, she realised that his telling her this much must have some relevance to why he had called to see her.

'The result being that you and Kit missed out?' she suggested.

Only she realised that what Gideon was more interested in talking about just then was Russell, and the woman Russell had married. 'The result being that Russell has grown perfectly content to let women run his life—his mother, his wife.' He ignored her question to state, 'He doesn't seem able to think for himself, though before Pamela came along and smelt his inheritance, he was quite capable of earning a living.'

'He doesn't have a job?'

'At the moment he doesn't need to work. His inheritance from his father kept him afloat to start with. Then, when he was twenty-five, he came into a small fortune left to him by my grandfather. He's thirty-two now and, I'd hazard a guess, has said goodbye to most of that fortune.'

'It—er—doesn't take much spending,' Ellena volunteered, knowing very little about it.

'Not when you're married to a woman who, cunning about everything else, gambles wildly on the stock exchange, it doesn't!' he said shortly. He paused, and then, to Ellena's amazement, added 'So, having gone through Russell's fortune, she's now after Kit's!'

'Kit's! Kit's fortune!' Ellena exclaimed.

'You didn't know?'

'He hasn't got any money!' She was certain of that. 'I know that for a fact! He had some, from your father, but that's gone and they're now living off Justine's money. Not that it matters to either of them—me neither—whose money it is, but Kit hasn't any now—' She broke off. Gideon was looking at her with something akin to a smile on his face. He was a man who didn't seem to smile a lot, though it was true he hadn't had a lot to smile about of late. But he was sort of smiling now, and, she owned, she liked the look of him.

'What a nice family you are,' he commented quietly, and she felt a flurry in the region of her heart and wasn't sure her cheeks didn't go a bit pink.

'I don't know about that... Well, yes, I do. Justine's lovely, and...'

'And her big sister's not so bad either.'

Oh, heck, he *did* have charm. 'You were saying that Kit has money, but...'

'Doesn't have now, but, like Russell, like I did, Kit inherits a third share of our grandfather's estate when he's twenty-five.'

'But—but, that's in about six months' time,' Ellena calculated.

'Exactly. Which is why, if I know my sister-in-law, and—' He broke off. 'I'm not giving up hope, Ellena, far from it,' he said gently, 'but we have to face the possibility that we may not see Kit and your sister again.'

She knew he was speaking only the truth. She nodded, and, when she thought she could speak, took up his suggestion, 'You think your sister-in-law will...'

'I know she will. By the time that six months is up, she'll have worked hard to ensure that she and Russell are legal guardians to Kit's child, and...'

'No!'

'And legal guardians to the child's inheritance.'

Ellena felt winded. 'But,' she gasped, 'she wouldn't be able to spend any of it!'

'You think not? Expenses, phoney and otherwise. Schools, holidays, clothes, new furnishings for her room...'

'Heavens!' Ellena could barely believe it. But, on thinking of that sour-expressioned woman, remembering her hostility, her coldness—not to mention remembering Justine saying that Pamela Langford had a nose for money and hadn't been able to offer her services fast enough in the context of it—she realised that believe it she could. 'I can't leave Violette there!' she exclaimed anxiously, ready to fight tooth and nail. 'It was just convenient at the time for Justine to leave her baby with your brother and his wife, but Justine wouldn't want her brought up by them—I just know it.'

'Neither would Kit. Which is why yesterday I checked out his writing desk hoping, now he has the responsibility of fatherhood, that he hadn't taken himself off on a ski-ing holiday without leaving some instruction with regard to his wishes for her.'

He meant a will, she knew he did, and realised that for all Gideon had said they should face the possibility of their siblings not returning, he was having an extremely tough time doing just that. So was she.

'You—' She broke off, her voice husky. She made a small coughing sound. 'You've been to his flat. You have a key?' The question was of small consequence, but it gave her the few seconds she needed to pull herself together after a weak moment.

'I'd all but forgotten I'd got it. To all intents and purposes the flat's Kit's...'

'You bought it for him after a bit of a wild party at your house while you were away?'

Gideon favoured her with that hint of a smile again. 'The flat is Kit's to live in,' he agreed, 'but mine to dispose of.'

'Ah!' she murmured, realising then that, though he loved his youngest brother very much, Gideon wasn't blind to the fact that, given the deeds to the property, he wouldn't have put it past Kit to sell the property if he had felt like it. 'Has he been very much of a headache to you?'

'What can I tell you? You've got one in the same mould.' He was right there, Ellena mused—it wasn't surprising Justine and Kit should have fallen in love with each other; they were equally as hair-raising. 'For the most part he's enjoyable to have around but I've had to come down hard on him on occasions.'

'The last time being six months ago?' she questioned.

'My oath, you're bright,' he answered, as if remembering that he'd told her he'd last visited Kit in the flat six months ago. 'I've spoken briefly to him over the phone since then, of course. But we've been a bit distant since I took him to task for being content to take and take, but not thinking of getting a job, or even of looking for one.'

'You couldn't find one for him in your organisation?'

'He had one—he doesn't like work. He gave it up.'

'I'm sorry,' Ellena said, realising that, for a man who worked so hard, it must have been increasingly difficult for him to find excuses for Kit.

'It's not your fault,' Gideon replied charmingly. 'I just feared he would go down the same shiftless road as Russell. Kit,' he added, 'has a fine brain if he troubled to use it.'

'He'll—er—perhaps he'll grow out of it.' They were both talking as if there was every chance that Kit had not perished.

'He's taking a long time about it!'

Ellena guessed that at close on twenty-five Gideon had already made great strides into a successful career. 'Perhaps…' she began, but left it there. Perhaps when Kit and Justine came back… Perhaps Kit would have grown up somewhat. Perhaps, perhaps. Abruptly she switched her thoughts away from 'perhaps'. That was in the future; she must concentrate on the present. 'Did you find anything, any instructions in Kit's desk?'

Gideon Langford shook his head. 'What I did find was a birth certificate in which Kit named himself as Violette Ellena's father.' His slate-grey eyes were steady on her when he added, 'The fact that the baby's parents thought well enough of you to give their child your name might well go towards being a deciding factor when my legal team take proceedings to...'

'Just a minute!' she halted him. She was, she felt, of normal and sometimes quite sharp intelligence. But she had lost him somewhere. Gideon had been talking of *her* name on Violette's birth certificate aiding in some way *his* application for guardianship! Ellena realised she must have missed something. 'You've as good as said,' she attempted to backtrack, 'that Russell and more particularly, his wife are out to get what money they can from—er—Kit's estate.' It hurt—but it was a possibility they might not come back.

'Russell will go along with whatever his wife tells him. And, as legal guardians of Kit's heir, they'd be in an ideal position to drain whatever they could in phoney expenses.'

'But—they won't get custody of her! I'm going to...'

'Russell is brother to the child's father. It was to him and his wife that Kit entrusted his daughter when he went on holiday,' Gideon pointed out levelly.

'Yes, but they wouldn't have taken Violette if they hadn't been handsomely paid to do so. They did it for the money! Justine as good as told me so! They—'

'Purely to cover expenses,' Gideon cut in. 'At least that's how Pamela will make a judge see it.'

'But-but…' She was floundering and they hadn't even got started yet! 'But she's not a blood relative! I am! I'm Violette's aunt—her mother's sister! Don't I…?'

'Her unmarried aunt,' Gideon tossed in.

Ellena wished he hadn't—it gave her something else to worry about. 'Do you think it will make a difference—my being unmarried?' she asked anxiously. Suddenly, though, she realised from *that* point of view Gideon Langford was in no better a position. 'Hang on—I thought you wanted Violette too!'

'I do,' he answered. 'Her unmarried uncle.'

Ellena hadn't slept much in the last forty-eight hours, so she blamed that for the fact that she had again lost Gideon somewhere. She admitted as much. 'What are you getting at?' she asked.

He shrugged. 'Merely that I, too, am the brother of the child's father.' Gideon paused, and studied her for a moment, those slate-grey eyes steady on her. Then, somehow deliberately, Ellena felt, he went on, 'According to the lawyers, my chances of being awarded the infant's guardianship would be greatly enhanced were I married.'

Ellena's mouth went dry. She was sure she didn't give a light that he might marry. But the thought that he and his wife—not withstanding that Russell and his wife might put in their claim—could jointly apply for Violette's care caused her to feel quite dreadful.

She swallowed hard. 'Are you going to get married?' she made herself ask.

That steady slate-grey-eyed look was still fixed on her. She met his gaze unwaveringly. But her jaw very near hit the floor when he replied coolly, 'I hope so. According to that same legal team, I would be more or less home and dry, were I, in fact, married—to the sister of the child's mother.'

Ellena's eyes shot wide. Open-mouthed, she stared at him.

CHAPTER THREE

ELLENA was still staring dumbfounded at Gideon after what seemed an age later. So *this* was why he had come to see her! She was only glad they were in her flat and not, as he'd offered, in some eating establishment. For in no way could she hide her absolute astonishment! He was saying nothing more. Having delivered his bombshell, he was silently watching, waiting to hear what she had to say about it.

'You're serious?' was what she did say when she found some breath.

'Never more so,' he replied evenly.

Ellena began to recover from her initial shock, but she still couldn't believe it. Then questions started queuing up that demanded answers. 'Let me get this right,' she began carefully. 'You're suggesting that, in order for you to gain legal guardianship of Justine and Kit's baby, you are prepared to marry me?'

'Got it in one,' Gideon answered—but it was about then, as the rest of her shock began to evaporate, that Ellena's brain started to function again.

80

'Er—forgive me for being dim, Gideon,' she apologised with polite sarcasm, 'but while it's extremely gallant of you to be prepared to marry me, could you give me one good reason why you think that I should so much as consider being prepared to marry you?'

Gideon Langford stared at her, was still staring at her when, unbelievably to her watching eyes, he remarked, 'Oh, my word, Ellena Spencer, I bet you're hell on earth once you get going!'

Her eyes mirrored her stupefaction, and it was her turn to stare. Her devil-may-care parents had occasionally been hell on earth. Justine frequently so. But quiet, studious and coping Ellena? Hell on earth—never! 'Untrue!' she retorted. And, since he hadn't answered her admittedly sarcastically-asked question, she unsarcastically rephrased it. 'Do you intend telling me why you think I should do this—er—marriage thing—for you?'

'You'd be doing it for yourself too,' Gideon answered seriously, and, while she failed to see how, he went on to explain, 'You want Violette. But, as things stand, you have about the same chance of getting her as me. I've thought about it a great deal, though in actual fact it didn't take long for me to see that I'd stand a much better chance of defeating Russell's cold and calculating wife if you and I joined forces.'

'Two against two, as opposed to one and one against two,' Ellena mused out loud. It was an insane idea, of course it was—and yet, she was a blood relative, Pamela wasn't; of the two married couples, wouldn't she and Gideon stand a better chance? Didn't it make sense? At least, it would if… 'You'd agree to my having Violette living with me?' she questioned abruptly, a beam of light suddenly appearing in the denseness of her darkness.

'Children are allowed here?' he returned before she could blink.

Clever hound! He thought he had her. Think again, Langford! 'No, but then I hadn't planned to take care of her here. I'd planned to buy a house in the country.' Pick the bones out of that! 'And—'

'Were we to marry, you'd naturally come and live with me,' Gideon cut her off. And, while she was thinking he could go and take a running jump, he was going on, 'For our—partnership to have any credence at all, we'd have to be seen to be living together, have to appear to be a loving couple, devoted to—'

'I get the picture,' she interrupted him quickly.

'Talking of love worries you?' he queried, seeming to be quite interested in her psyche.

'Obviously you do it every day!' she snapped crisply—and couldn't believe it when, for the first time, she heard him laugh, a short amused bark of laughter.

'As a point of fact, I don't,' he commented easily. But he was serious when he went on, 'It's important that no one suspects the true reason for our marriage.' She hadn't said she'd marry him yet! 'It's important we look as though we married for love.'

Ellena owned that she was not the madcap one of the family and never would be. Yet to marry Gideon Langford as he suggested would, in her view, be even more madcap than anything Justine had ever done. 'Couldn't we just pretend to be engaged?' she wriggled.

Gideon shook his head. 'No. It wouldn't do.' He turned her suggestion down flat. 'Russell's wife will be watching from every angle. Once she realises her get-rich plans are looking decidedly rocky, she'll stop at nothing.'

'She sounds dreadful!'

'Believe me, there are women like her in the world. Anyhow, you've met her!'

That she had. Without Justine's comments about the avaricious woman, Ellena, from her own observations, saw Pamela Langford as a cold and nasty type. Certainly not a type to whom she would entrust anything so precious as her niece—which was, of course, what the whole of this was about. Pamela Langford, with or without a temporary nanny to take care of Violette, was not going to have charge of her!

'Marriage—could be the answer,' she agreed slowly.

'It is,' he stated firmly. 'The two basic criteria are that we need to be married, and you need to be living in my home.'

Ellena tried to look beyond the facts that to marry Gideon Langford and to live in his house were the last things she wanted to do. She wanted Violette to be brought up with love. 'Er…' He waited. Thinking of love activated her imagination into the realms of the loving relationship she would supposedly have with him. Grief—they'd only met two days ago! 'We'd—um—have to make believe it was love at first sight,' she spoke her thoughts. 'For anyone to believe it, we'd have to pretend we were attracted from—' She broke off. As he'd earlier spotted, she wasn't very comfortable talking of love. And yet she continued when the next rapid thought swiftly landed, 'What if we fall in love…?' Her voice faded when his right eyebrow ascended aloft. 'With other people, I mean!' she finished crossly.

'You do like to meet crises head-on—precipitate them before they happen,' he drawled, and that annoyed her some more.

'You can talk!' she erupted. 'You had your lawyers wiping the dust off their law books before we'd barely landed yesterday!'

Gideon inclined his head to acknowledge, *Touché*, but did her the courtesy of answering her question. 'In the event of either of us falling in love, you and I will amicably discuss that situation when it arises. But the child's interests must come first.'

'I wouldn't argue about that,' Ellena agreed.

'You agree, then—we marry?'

'No, no,' she said, panic attacking her. 'Hold it a minute! You've had all night to sort out the pros and cons of what you propose. There are a dozen and one things I need to have clear first.'

'Such as?'

'Look, you've only just dropped this on me, I can't think of all I need to know at once!' she protested. He did not look impressed. She felt forced to go on. 'Well, for one thing, I was thinking of having a nanny take care of Violette Monday to Friday while I'm at work. How would any judge view that, do you think?' Her question had little to do with any plans to marry, she realised that, but it was something that had worried her, and had just sort of come out.

'I think your industry would be viewed far more favourably than the indolent lifestyle of my brother and his wife,' Gideon answered un-hesitatingly.

That cheered her, but though that one very big worry was now somewhat lessened, she wasn't very comfortable with the next question that sprang to mind—it was a very gigantic one from where she was seeing it. 'This marriage...' she began, and got stuck before she started.

Whether Gideon had any idea of what she wanted to ask she had no idea, but she did men-tally thank him that his look softened, and his tone was gently encouraging when he prompted quietly, 'Don't be afraid, Ellena. Ask whatever bothers you.'

Thus invited, she took a long breath, and plunged. 'This marriage... Oh, grief, I wish I knew more about men and their... But, what with studying and keeping an eye on what Justine was getting up...' This was ridiculous, she fumed, cross with herself, with him. It was all his fault—he had put her in this position and she shouldn't have had to explain anything about herself, for goodness' sake! 'I'm not hav-

ing a proper marriage with you!' she told him
bluntly. 'Not that I've said I will at all yet,' she
tacked on hastily.

'By "proper", you mean consummated?' he
queried—with not a sign of a blush about him.

Not so Ellena; had she been answering, she
might have dressed it up a little, but not him!
Though it did come down to that very thing.
'That's what I mean,' she agreed, feeling very
pink in the face.

'Do you have a steady boyfriend?' he asked.

'What's that got to do with anything?' she
flared. He knew she hadn't. She felt sure he
knew—did that make her a lesser mortal?

'I wouldn't put it past my sister-in-law to
have you followed.' Gideon revealed what it
had to do with his question.

'Oh!' Ellena exclaimed—heavens, was he
two streets in front of everyone else? Ellena
owned that, up to now, though mainly by
choice, her dates had been few and far between.
But should some hired private detective follow
her if she dated someone, then Gideon's sister-
in-law would soon have evidence she could use
to show their 'love marriage' was not what it
should be, that their home was an unstable one
in which to rear a child. 'There's no one special,' Ellena owned, and, wondering why some

detective should follow her and not him, 'How about you? Are you seeing anyone?'

'I'm resting,' he replied, with such a look of mock sorrow that she had the strongest desire to laugh. She glanced to the floor for a moment so he shouldn't see the amusement in her eyes, but looked up again when, his tone serious, he stated, 'While we were married we'd have to agree not to date anyone else.'

'How long would it last?' she asked and, some imp of mischief catching her unawares, added, 'And could you ''rest'' that long?'

His answer was to grin—oh, heavens, how it changed him! She saw in him a kind of wickedness she had never noticed before, and for the first time saw something of Kit there too. Perhaps he had been a lot more like Kit at one time. Perhaps, before his father's death and before he'd had to take on the responsibilities of running and then expanding Langford Engineering, Gideon had been as happy-go-lucky as Kit. That Gideon took his responsibilities most seriously was beyond doubt, given the facts that not only was Langford Engineering the thriving concern it had become, but also that Gideon was so determined to have responsibility for his brother's child, that he was prepared to go through a marriage ceremony to help achieve that aim.

'So?' she asked when he still hadn't answered her question about how long the marriage would last. 'It could go on for years!'

'I'm doing nothing special for the next year or two,' Gideon answered. 'By which time, if Kit and Justine haven't returned,' he inserted gravely, 'the child will be in a more stable and kind environment, and we can review what we both want for ourselves, and for her.'

'Amicably,' she inserted, borrowing his word.

That hint of a smile touched the corners of his mouth again. 'How does that sound?' he asked.

Ellena, save for getting on with her career, had nothing special planned for the next year or two either. 'I've no quarrel with that,' she answered.

'Good,' he replied, going on, 'So, the ground rules are that neither of us dates anyone else until we're certain my sister-in-law has given up.'

'There's no other choice.' She could see that.

'So you agree—we marry?'

Whoa, there! Panic started to throw spiteful, tummy-churning darts at her. Ellena had the feeling of being hurtled along. Yes, she could make quick decisions, but this wasn't a new coat she was buying, or a client about whom she was making decisions in her professional capacity. Naturally she was prepared to devote all her energies and time to Justine's baby, but to tie herself up with Gideon Langford for a couple of years—oh, pray God, Justine was all right and came home!—was something she wanted a little more time to consider.

'Do you do everything at a gallop?' she questioned, a shade aggressively, it was true.

'I don't have time to delay,' he retorted. 'I want everything cut and dried when next I contact my sister-in-law.' Ellena looked across at him. He was trustworthy, she knew that. And he wanted what, in his view, was only the best for his infant niece; she knew that too. But, as she stared at him, his look softened again, 'You'd be able to carry on with your work, just the same,' he assured her. 'I'd engage a nanny...'

'Only from Monday to Friday,' she interrupted him quickly. 'I'd want to take care of Violette myself at weekends. Let her know she's much loved—' She broke off, afraid she was revealing too much of the emotion she felt. 'It sounds good,' she admitted. 'There has to be a snag—oh!'

'You've just thought of one?'

'I've been talking as though our winning custody of Violette is a foregone conclusion. But—what if we went so far as to get married only for some judge to rule against our claim for Violette?'

'We appeal!' Gideon replied unhesitatingly. It was a rare occasion, she was sure, but he allowed her a peep into his own emotions as he revealed, 'Kit means more to me than allowing his child to be reared in a home where, were it not for her monetary value, she is unwanted.'

Ellena went along with that, all the way, and felt more than a little emotional herself just then. But, with difficulty, she made herself be practical. 'And if any appeal fails?' she asked.

He looked at her steadily. 'The marriage would be annulled,' he decreed.

She'd go along with that too. She tried to think if there was anything else she should ask, but felt she had covered everything. 'When do you need to know by?' she queried, guessing from his statement that he wanted everything cut and dried he'd require her answer sooner rather than later.

But she stared at him witless when he replied, 'As soon as I have your answer I'll apply for a special licence. We can be married by this time next week.'

'Good heavens!' she exclaimed, and darts of panic started to attack again. 'Justine and Kit could be back from their holiday in two or three weeks!'

'While I don't want to accept it either—they may not be,' he stated heavily. 'And then I'll have given Pamela Langford two or three weeks head start!'

So be it. Ellena gave a shaky sigh. 'May I sleep on it?' she asked.

His answer was to stand up. Ellena left her chair too, and was in receipt of a direct no-nonsense sort of look from his steady slate-grey eyes as he informed her, 'I'll ring you first thing in the morning.' He delayed only long enough to take her home phone number, then he left her—with a whole lot of thinking to do.

She paced the floor, going over every-thing—and tried to be strong when she thought of Justine. She swallowed down tears and made herself think only of Violette. She remembered the money-grabbing Pamela Langford—who had no love for the infant—and Ellena knew that she was going to have Violette in her safe keeping and caring, or die in the attempt. Which suddenly made her realise that if to marry Gideon Langford increased her chances by over twenty-five percent, which surely it must, then marrying him was not the gigantic hurdle it had seemed at first.

Ellena went and showered and got into bed, but lay wide awake with too much on her mind to give sleep a chance. How could she sleep?

At midnight she got out of bed and made herself a warm drink. At three o'clock she left her bed again and put the kettle on for a cup of tea. She sat down at the kitchen table and tried to analyse what—apart from the very real fear that she might never see Justine again—she was so worried about.

She wanted Violette. Fact. She stood a much better chance of getting her if she threw in her lot with Gideon. Fact. What did she know about him? He was trustworthy, honourable and, with all he had going for him, would, whether she married him or did not marry him, fight with all he had to gain guardianship of his brother's child—which meant that she would have to fight him too.

Ellena didn't doubt he would put up a tremendous battle. Wasn't he—bachelor of the year—prepared to go so far as to give up his freedom in that fight? Would she do less? No, by thunder, she wouldn't!

At four o'clock, realising that it wasn't as though she hated him, for goodness' sake, and, thank heavens, she didn't have to love him either, Ellena went and found his phone number. She knew she wasn't going to get any sleep until she'd got this first hurdle settled. And, on the basis that since it was his call to her stating the proposed merger that had kept her sleepless, she didn't see why he shouldn't be sleepless too.

She dialled and, despite not being the harebrained one in the family, saw nothing at all wrong in getting someone out of bed at four in the morning. Gideon Langford had said he'd ring her first thing—so she'd saved him the bother.

The phone rang out only briefly and was answered almost immediately. 'Gideon?'

'Couldn't you sleep either?' His voice was even, calm. She pictured him, tall, good-looking—she was going to marry him!

She swallowed and, while praying that Justine would come back—come back early—and that she would not have to take the colossal step of marrying him, she, who had not done a reckless thing during the last five years, took the plunge. 'Do I need to take a day off work?'

'Make it Thursday,' he answered. Ellena put the phone down. Today was Saturday. She had a lot to do—she was getting married on Thursday!

After a few hours' sleep, Ellena got up and pattered into the kitchen. She put the kettle to boil, and while making a cup of tea—and while still feeling somewhat shaken when she realised that she had, at four o'clock this morning, agreed to marry a man she barely knew—she set about being practical.

Strangely, though, when practicalities suggested that, since she would be leaving her flat for the duration of her marriage, she should spend the day sorting through what to pack and what to leave, she discovered she didn't want to do anything of the sort.

She was getting married on Thursday, for goodness' sake! Suddenly Ellena discovered that the practical side of her nature was up against a recently awakened incautious side. Harebrained it might be, but she wanted something nice to wear at her wedding. She had another four days in which to sort out her clothes!

Ellena spent the day shopping. She had long legs and the warm, blue, above-the-knee dress she purchased showed them off to advantage. With the dress came a matching boxy jacket, which complemented the colour of her eyes perfectly.

Naturally, even though Violette would not be at the wedding, Ellena bought her a dress too.

She let herself into her flat, experiencing an urge to go and see the baby, to hold and love her. The phone rang.

Ellena dropped down her carriers, hope in her heart that Justine, an alive and well Justine, had taken it into her head to give her a call.

She picked up the phone, forgetting completely that Justine had never thought to telephone when she'd been away on holiday before. 'Hello,' she said huskily, emotion getting to her.

'You've been crying!' Gideon Langford accused.

'No, I haven't!' Ellena denied sharply, any stiffening she needed there at his tone. Then, feeling she had overreacted, 'I thought you might be Justine,' she explained, and at once felt foolish; grief, he was an all-practical male!

There was a pause, and Ellena knew that she really liked him when he answered sympathetically, 'It's unbearable, I know.'

'You've heard nothing from Austria, I suppose?'

'Not a word,' he answered, and, not giving her time to dwell on sad thoughts, he continued, 'At a guess, I'd say you've spent the day packing.'

Oh, heck—he thought she was as practical as she had thought she was herself. Somehow she didn't like that. Somehow she wanted to be non-practical. She'd had years of being practical.

'You'd guess wrong,' she answered, and, because all at once it seemed unbelievable, she questioned, 'Are we really getting married on Thursday?'

'We are,' he assured her straight away. 'Which is part of the reason for this call. In the cause of our "love at first sight" engagement, it's occurred to me we should be spending a little more time together.'

'I hadn't thought of that,' she confessed.

'You're slipping,' he answered, his tone light. Grief, what did he think she was? Some mastermind? 'I wondered if you'd like to come and see your future home tomorrow? If you do have anything packed you could bring it with you.'

'I suppose going to see Violette tomorrow is out of the question?'

'I'm afraid so. Trust me on this, Ellena,' he said gently. 'I promise you—once we have our certificate of marriage things will move fast. Hold back until then.'

She gave a shaky sigh. 'Roll on Thursday!'

'That's what I like—an eager bride!'

'Get you!' she scoffed—but found she was laughing, which, she realised, was far better than the near tearful state she'd been in at the start of his call.

'I'll pick you up tomorrow at—'

'No need for that,' she cut him off pleasantly. 'Just give me your address, tell me what time, and I'll be there.'

Gideon told her how to get to Oakvale, his home, and Ellena gave him the information he requested which he thought he might need to make their marriage application.

After his call she went and hung up her new dress and jacket. Her new outfit wasn't exactly bridal, she had to own, but neither was it funereal. She had to believe Justine was alive. She couldn't bear to think that she wasn't.

Ellena could not remember ever being so interested in clothes before. But the very next morning she found she was in a dilemma about what to wear to go to Sunday lunch at Gideon's home.

By ten-thirty that morning she was dressed in a fine wool suit of pale mustard, with her blonde hair silky about her shoulders. She had been going to pull it back in the chignon which she sometimes wore but, on thinking about it, would any newly engaged woman go and meet her 'love at first sight' fiancé with her hair dressed so formally?

Ellena pulled up on the wide drive of Oakvale and took a deep breath. In acres of its own grounds, the Georgian house with its many windows was larger than she had anticipated—and beautiful. Oh, heavens, she was going to live here!

She got out of her car—and looked up to see Gideon had left the house and was crossing the gravel to meet her. 'Ellena,' he smiled and, reaching her, took hold of her upper arms. She stared at him, startled. 'My housekeeper is extremely loyal, but you never know who's watching. May I?' he enquired, and before she could begin to think what he was about, he bent his head—and touched his lips to hers.

They were walking across the drive to the open front door of the house before she had her head anywhere near together again. She had been kissed before, but—given that Gideon's mouth on hers had been but a brief meeting of lips—never had she felt so all over the place afterwards!

Her thoughts were still tangled up with the very far-fetched notion of newspaper photographers with telephoto lenses—and also with the fact she had packed a suitcase and left it in her car but had been too witless, after Gideon's light kiss, to remember it—when he escorted her inside his home.

'Your house is beautiful.' She felt she should say something.

'I think so,' Gideon answered. 'Let's go to the kitchen and say hello to Mrs Morris. She and her husband, with outside help, keep the place going for me.'

'Have you lived here long?' Ellena asked, going through a large hall towards the rear of the house with him.

'I was brought up here. It's the family home,' he answered. 'I had my own place after university, but purchased the house from my mother when she remarried.'

He really must love it, Ellena realised. 'Your mother lives in the Bahamas, doesn't she? Does she know about—?' She broke off as they halted by a door.

'We're in daily contact,' Gideon revealed, and while Ellena's heart went out to Kit's poor mother, who must be suffering agonies over him, Gideon opened the door and guided her into the kitchen where he introduced his plump, fiftyish housekeeper, Mrs Morris.

'How do you do?' Ellena smiled, shaking the housekeeper by the hand.

'I hope you and Mr Langford will be very happy,' Mrs Morris beamed.

'Oh!' Ellena exclaimed, startled, and knew she was handling this first outside reference to their planned marriage very badly. She was, she owned, absolutely hopeless at deception.

But smooth wasn't the word for it! Gideon was there before she could draw another breath. 'I hope you'll forgive me, Ellena, but since you're going to be mistress of Oakvale from next Thursday, I felt you wouldn't mind if I shared our good news with Mrs Morris.'

'Of course.' Ellena smiled, refusing an offer of coffee. A minute or so later, they crossed back over the hall to Gideon's drawing room, Ellena trying to cope with the notion that— hopefully very briefly—she was going to be mistress of this very beautiful house.

'Would you like something to drink?' Gideon offered as she stood on the thick-pile carpet admiring the elegant yet comfortable room.

'I hadn't better. I'll be driving later,' she declined.

A moment later she was staring at him in amazement when, pausing to take something from the drawer of a small antique table, he came over to her and, opening what she now saw was a ring box, said, 'You'd better have this.'

She took the ring from him purely because, when he pushed it at her, it seemed impolite not to take it. 'What is it?'

'Your engagement ring.'

Her glance flew from the diamond solitaire up to his steady grey gaze. 'I...' I don't want it, she had been going to say, but they weren't doing this for her, or for either of them, but to ensure that Violette had the best. 'Is it r-real?' she asked—never had she met such a man for scattering her wits. 'The diamond, I mean.'

'Would I give my fiancée anything less?' he mocked.

'I'll let you have it back,' she promised. 'After... When...'

Gideon smiled; with just the two of them there, and with no one to witness it, he smiled. 'An honest woman!' he teased.

'Believe me, there are women like that in the world,' she teasingly quoted one of his comments back at him.

'And I've just met one,' he said softly, admiring of her honesty, his glance going from her lovely eyes, over her exquisite bone structure and creamy skin, down to linger on her sweetly curving mouth. Taking the ring from her, he slid it gently home on her engagement finger.

Her legs seemed to go to jelly. With the greatest of difficulty, she dragged the practical side of her up from somewhere. 'Talking of suitcases,' she said, turning away, 'I've one very large one in my car.'

He laughed; she heard him. As if he enjoyed her, he gave a short laugh. Perhaps, if they both kept their sense of humour, they might not fare so badly together after all—be it longer than they presently anticipated.

'You didn't lock your car; I'll go and get your case in,' he said, and was off, leaving her to dwell on the fact that her legs had gone decidedly weak a second or two ago.

He was away some minutes and, by the time he returned, with no suitcase in sight, Ellena felt much more in one piece. 'I've taken your case up to your room,' he informed her. 'Your room' somehow made her feel that she belonged. 'And Mrs Morris tells me lunch is ready.'

Lunch was a superbly cooked meal and Gideon was good company throughout, Ellena discovered. 'That was delicious,' she said, as she finished the last of her home-made apple pie. 'I think I'm going to enjoy living here,' she added. He had been so totally charming, she didn't want to let her side down. Though, lest Gideon thought that she might be staking some claim, 'Temporarily,' she tacked on quickly. Gracious, he knew, and was interested in, much more sophisticated types, if he was thinking of anything of a *permanent* nature, and—good heavens, what was wrong with her?—she didn't want him to be interested in her! Perish such a thought!

Ellena did not visit Gideon's home again before her wedding day. She wore her engagement ring to work on Monday and, because she was terrified that the least little slip might endanger her hopes that she and Gideon would have custody of Violette, she was scared to tell even Andrea that love didn't enter into her engagement with Gideon.

'May I see you?' she asked Andrea when she arrived at the office, hoping because of the respect she had for Andrea that she wasn't going to have to tell her too many lies.

'Of course. Come in and close the door,' Andrea agreed at once. 'Any news?' she asked as they both sat down.

Ellena knew Andrea meant Justine and Kit. 'None,' she answered, and straight away got down to the reason for wanting to see her. 'The thing is, I'd rather like to have a couple of days off,' she began, for authenticity's sake realising that she'd better take Friday off as well.

'You're going back to Aust—' Andrea began, then, her observant gaze catching sight of Ellena's left hand, she stopped abruptly. 'You're engaged!' she exclaimed. 'I didn't even know you were going steady! When did this happen?' More questions seemed to be on the way when Andrea suddenly stopped. 'Who is he?' she slowed down to ask. 'And does he know how lucky he is?' she added warmly.

'Oh, Andrea. I—He...' Ellena began helplessly, then seemed to get the energy she needed to explain, 'It happened very quickly, but we—need each other.' It wasn't a lie. Without each other, her chance and Gideon's chance of being guardians to Violette were greatly reduced. 'Gideon Langford and I—'

'Gideon Langford!' Andrea cut in, her surprise evident. Quickly, though, she recovered. 'Of course, you met him through your sister,' she said gently, assuming—something which hadn't occurred to Ellena—that, through Justine and Kit, she and Gideon had known each other some while! Even perhaps that, having been much in each other's company of late, they had realised their love for each other. In any event, there was nothing but a warm sincerity in her tones when Andrea wished her well.

'The thing is, we see little point in waiting. We're—um—getting married on Thursday. Just a small private ceremony because of...' She had no need to go on.

'Oh, my dear, I'm so pleased! I've worried so for you. But with Gideon Langford to care for you.' She stopped there, as a rather unpalatable thought suddenly came to her. 'You're not leaving? You haven't come to give me your resignation?'

Relief washed over Ellena that this interview had gone far better than she had anticipated. She even managed to look happy as she replied, 'No, of course not. I love working. Love working here. I just want Thursday and Friday off, that's all.'

The first thing Ellena did when she went to her own office was to put through a call to her solicitors and cancel her appointment with Mr Ollerenshaw. Gideon seemed to have everything sorted—she could fault none of his, or his lawyers', logic.

She hurried home from work that evening, hoping against hope that a second card from Justine had arrived. But there was nothing in the post from Austria.

Quite unexpectedly, Gideon stopped by her flat at around seven. She thought she was glad to see him. 'Did you tell them you wouldn't be in Thursday?' he asked, standing in her kitchen with her while she made him a cup of coffee.

She flicked a glance to him, feeling amused that it didn't occur to him she'd have to *ask* for time off from her work. 'I did,' she answered, and felt just a tinge discomforted when she revealed, 'I thought I'd better have Friday off as well—er—for the look of the thing,' she added, glancing quickly from him.

Naturally, he caught on straight away. 'Would you like to go away on a honeymoon?' he enquired politely.

'No!' She knocked that idea firmly on the head.

'My charm must be slipping,' he drawled, and, for all she gave him a speaking look, she liked him when he grinned, especially when he confided, 'Funny thing. I've arranged to be absent from work, too, on Friday. Had time to pack anything else? I can take it with me if you've got another case ready.'

She did not see him on Tuesday, but he phoned on Wednesday evening, just as she was starting to panic about what she was on the eve of doing. 'I'm glad you rang!' she said without thinking.

'Problem?'

'Only with me,' she confessed. 'Are we doing the right thing? Getting married, I mean.'

There was a slight pause the other end, then he replied tautly, 'I don't think I'd ever forgive you if you stood me up.'

Was he joking? She couldn't tell. 'Jilted on the registry office steps,' she said lightly—as if anyone would *dare* to jilt him! 'I'm sorry,' she apologised, 'It's just—well, I suppose I'm getting the jitters and need a bit of reassurance.'

'So how about—divided, and single, we each have a very poor chance of having the right to guard one Violette Ellena Langford. United, and married, our chances of caring for that little girl are far better than the other claimants'.'

'So, put a carnation in your buttonhole,' she answered, and suddenly felt a whole heap better.

To her surprise, Ellena slept well that night. She was up early, though. They were marrying at three that afternoon. Since they could hardly leave after the marriage ceremony in two separate vehicles, Gideon had arranged for her to be picked up and driven to the registry office. On Monday morning Gideon would drive her to her flat, where she would pick up her car and go to her office. From there, on Monday evening, she would drive to her new home, Oakvale.

Save for the fact that nerves were again attacking her, everything went as planned. The chauffeur-driven limousine arrived and Ellena was certain by then that what she was doing was right. She felt nervous only because, well, as she told herself, it wasn't every day that a girl got married, or to such a man as Gideon. She was met by him at ten to three that afternoon.

He came close up to her and—purely because other people were about, she was sure—he murmured, 'I knew you were beautiful. Today you look sensational.' And, lightly, he touched his lips to hers.

What could she do? She smiled. Blow anyone watching—Gideon had made her feel good. He gave her roses, and then snapped one bloom off and put it in his buttonhole. She laughed.

He looked at her. 'It will be all right, I promise,' he whispered—and just then a camera flash went off, and she realised some of the press were there.

The ceremony went without a hitch—she had been afraid she might develop a stammer or, worse, lose her voice entirely. Their witnesses were a couple of directors from Gideon's firm who, possibly because they were aware of the tragedy that might have befallen his brother and her sister, were both compassionate and congratulatory, but in a controlled way.

Ellena and Gideon posed briefly for press photos after the ceremony, then she and the man she had just married were in his car, alone, and driving away. Ellena transferred her engagement ring from its temporary home on her right hand to pair it with her wedding band on the third finger of her left hand. She caught Gideon giving her a glance.

'That's two rings I owe you,' she commented lightly.

'You amaze me!' he declared.

There wasn't any answer to that. 'I know,' she said, and felt like smiling. His eyes were back on the road but, from the way the corner of his mouth twitched, she had an idea that he was suppressing a smile too.

Her smile went deep into hiding, however, when, on reaching his home, and having been warmly congratulated by both Mr and Mrs Morris, Gideon suggested that she might like to change.

Ellena hadn't thought about it, but guessed this was his way of saying he would show her where she would be sleeping and where she could wash her hands. She went up the wide staircase with him, a thought only then striking her. Gideon had spoken of her room. Oh, heavens, did it matter that Mrs Morris, his housekeeper, would soon know that they would not be sharing a bed?

Ellena did not have long to worry about it, however, because, moving to the right-hand side of the landing, Gideon escorted her to a door, which he opened, and stood back. Ellena went in.

It was a large airy bedroom, with a large double bed, elegant furniture, ankle-deep cream carpet matching the cream curtains. 'You'll be comfortable here, but if there's anything you want to change, or need, remember that you're mistress here now.'

'Oh, Gideon, how nice,' she said, thinking it very kind of him, but if Justine came home soon she wouldn't have time to change anything. Not that the decor needed changing anyway.

There were another two doors in the room, to the bathroom, she judged, and dressing room. Wrong, she discovered as, unbeknown to her, Gideon had been watching her. 'That's your bathroom,' he said, indicating one door, 'and that,' he said, indicating the other, 'is the door to my room.'

'Your room!' Startled, she stared at him, her blue eyes wide. 'There's no key!' she observed.

'Now don't panic. Just stay calm and listen,' Gideon urged.

'You said this marriage wouldn't be con-con…'

'Just because I'm sleeping next door doesn't mean I'm going to lustfully charge in and claim my conjugal rights!'

'You tell me what it means, then!' she flew heatedly. 'You must have half a dozen bedrooms you can use, or one I could have either if…'

'Spare me from outraged virgins!' Gideon threw up a prayer, while she would have liked to have thrown up a hand—and hit him. 'See here, I've told you Mrs Morris's loyalty is without question. What is questionable is the loyalty of any unknown newcomer to this household.'

'Newcomer?' Did he mean her? He couldn't, could he?

Apparently not. 'Nanny!' he reminded her. 'We have to have a nanny, don't we?'

Ellena calmed down somewhat. 'We do,' she agreed.

'A nanny who, whether we like it or not, may be alone in this part of the house at any time of the day while we're out of it.'

'You think she may pry into our sleeping arrangements?'

'Most probably not. But I'm not jeopardising my claim to guardianship of Kit's daughter by taking that risk. I've no intention of it getting back to Russell and his wife that the newly married couple sleep at opposite ends of the house.'

'You think Pamela would go so far as to question our nanny?' Ellena couldn't believe it! Although, recalling Pamela Langford...

'I doubt she'd do it personally, but she'd pay to have someone sniff round for any useful information.'

'It sounds incredible!'

'There's big money to be had—Pamela wants it,' Gideon said succinctly.

Ellena's thoughts went straight to the baby. Poor little love. She just couldn't leave her with that woman; she just couldn't. Justine couldn't have been thinking straight to have left Violette with Pamela to start with.

Suddenly, then, it seemed secondary to panic that Gideon might want to lustfully make a call on her—when clearly he did not. Indeed, he had never—apart from a couple of extremely light kisses when there was a chance they were being observed—made, done, or said anything to give her the smallest qualm about such a matter.

And, in any case, he could as easily make a call on her via the main door to her room as the communicating door.

'I'm making a fuss about nothing, aren't I?' she apologised, feeling a little shamefaced.

'The fault is mine,' he took the blame handsomely. 'I'd intended to show you your room last Sunday, then got to thinking it might worry you and that perhaps it would be better to wait.' He looked at her from his steady grey eyes. 'You're not worried now?' he asked.

Having kicked up a fuss needlessly once, she was anxious not to make a fool of herself a second time. 'Not a bit!' she assured him stoutly.

'May I then suggest that while, naturally, the communicating door will remain closed at night—' Ellena felt a hint peeved—to hear him talk, anyone would think *his* honour was at stake—he should be so lucky! '—I'd appreciate, assuming you're the last one to leave for the office, if you'd open it, and leave it so during the day.'

'To show that...'

'While to sleep separately is perhaps not too unusual, it might be as well for us to be seen—should word escape—to have an... intimate...relationship.'

'Of course,' she quickly agreed.

'Good,' he said. 'Now, I'll leave you to settle in while I make a phone call. I've an idea Mrs Morris may have gone to town on our dinner this evening.'

Mrs Morris had made a wonderful meal, Ellena discovered, when that evening Gideon knocked on her door and they went down the stairs. As before, Gideon was a splendid host, talking on any subject but the one she was most interested in: their niece. He had said that once they had their marriage certificate things would move fast in that direction. So, what was happening?

Realising she was being impatient—for Heaven's sake, the ink was barely dry on that certificate yet—Ellena decided that tomorrow she and Gideon must have an in-depth talk about it. She had come close to upsetting him when she'd objected to his easy access to her room. Much better to leave it until the next day.

Ellena had no idea why she didn't want to upset Gideon twice in one day, but, looking across to him as the meal came to a close, she knew only that she preferred him in this friendly mood of companionship, than when he was looking as if he was about to get tough.

'That was wonderful,' she stated, and, placing her napkin on the table, she continued, 'Would it be all right if I went and thanked Mrs Morris? She must have worked awfully hard.'

'How sweet you are,' Gideon murmured, and, standing up, 'Come on, I'll go with you.' Ellena wasn't sure how she felt about 'sweet', though supposed it was preferable to sour.

It had seemed natural to Ellena to seek Mrs Morris out, but the housekeeper seemed delighted that she had troubled to do so. 'It was a pleasure,' Mrs Morris beamed at their thanks, and Ellena, with Gideon at her side, left her and went back to the main part of the house.

At the door of the drawing room, however, Ellena decided she would quite like to go up to her room. 'I think I'll leave you to it,' she offered pleasantly.

Gideon halted. 'Had enough of my company for one day?' he teased.

'That would be a first,' she laughed.

'You've got me all wrong!' he protested.

'You don't have women by the score? You don't subscribe to the love 'em and leave 'em school of thought?'

'I'll have you know, madam,' he countered, 'that I'm a happily married man.'

That 'happily' pleased her. 'Goodnight,' she said quickly.

He caught a hold of her hand, the teasing and banter suddenly gone from his eyes. 'Goodnight, Ellena,' he said softly, and, with no one there at all to observe, he bent down and gently kissed her lips. And, as he straightened, he looked deep into her warm, if perhaps slightly confused eyes, and added, 'Thank you for marrying me today.' Then he took a step back. 'I'll see you at breakfast,' he said.

Ellena turned away, her feet seeming to make automatically for the stairs. It seemed odd to her that she hadn't protested when he kissed her.

Though no odder, surely, she thought whimsically, than the fact that she should go to bed on her honeymoon night with her husband's words 'I'll see you at breakfast' ringing in her ears!

CHAPTER FOUR

ELLENA slept soundly that night. She'd heard Gideon moving about in the next-door room before sleep claimed her. But, though she had thought she would feel a little on edge, come night time, that he was close by in one bedroom while she lay in another, she had to admit that she'd felt more secure by his near presence than anything else!

She heard a noise, and realised that it was muffled sounds from next door that had awakened her. She heard the soft thud of his door closing and, remembering Gideon's parting remark that he would see her at breakfast, realised she'd better get a move on.

Leaving her bed, Ellena quickly showered and dressed. She had little knowledge of what a bride might wear for breakfast on the first day of her honeymoon but, since she wasn't going to work that day, considered that tailored trousers and a light sweater would fit the bill.

From force of habit she made her bed, and was on her way out of the room when she suddenly remembered the communicating door.

Oops, she was supposed to leave it open! She changed direction and, just in case Gideon had returned to his room while she was in the shower, she tapped lightly on the wood panelling.

No answer! She opened the door a little way, then thought, Stupid! and pushed it wide. Gideon's room, though large, was not as large as hers, she saw. Oh, now, wasn't that kind of him, to give her the larger room? True, it might not be for very long, but he needn't have... Her attention was drawn to his large double bed, as yet unmade, and a small gurgle of laughter erupted. She had played her part by opening the door wide, Gideon had played his by putting a decided dent in the pillow beside the one he had used.

Gideon was in conversation with Mrs Morris when Ellena entered the breakfast room, but he broke off, rising to his feet when he saw her. 'You made it while the coffee's still hot,' he greeted her, and Ellena, about to greet him back with a pleasant 'Good morning', halted just in time, feeling herself go a shade pink as she realised that in normal circumstances a bride would very probably already have given her husband a much less formal greeting.

She smiled at him instead. 'Good morning, Mrs Morris,' she addressed the housekeeper, and realised that Gideon wasn't the only one to have noticed her suddenly pinkened cheeks when the woman answered her greeting, her expression going dreamy and understanding.

Gideon was holding out a chair at the table for her. 'What are you having for breakfast?' he enquired solicitously.

She was glad to take the seat, and, as Gideon sat down beside her, Ellena answered, 'May I have some cereal and a banana, if there is one?' Mrs Morris went smilingly on her way to arrange it. But Ellena was still feeling a shade awkward. 'I never used to blush until I met you!' she laid the blame at his door.

'What did I say?' Gideon asked, but there was a light of mischief in his eyes when he added, 'Mrs Morris was positively enchanted.'

Ellena, for all she supposed she had instigated this conversation, had already had quite enough of it. 'What sort of thing do you normally do when you have a day off?' she enquired to change the subject. 'And don't answer that if you'd rather not!' she added quickly, as she realised that there was every good chance that he spent most of his free time wining, dining and—whatever—with the opposite sex.

He looked back at her as if she amused him—she wasn't very sure how she felt about that. 'Apart from a holiday now and then, I can't remember the last time I had a day off,' he answered.

'Diplomatic!' she murmured, her lips twitching.

'You really do have a wrong opinion of me,' he answered smoothly. And at that juncture, into that pleasant atmosphere, Mrs Morris came in bearing a tray with everything Ellena required.

She thanked her, and as the housekeeper left the breakfast room it suddenly came to Ellena what she wanted to do with her own day off. 'I don't suppose...' she began without thinking further—and stopped.

'You don't suppose?' Gideon encouraged.

'Forget it.' She shook her head. 'It's an enormous cheek.'

'Now I really *am* intrigued.'

Oh, help. She was making too much of it. Wishing that she had never opened her mouth, yet aware that Gideon was waiting, she felt forced to go on. 'Well, I—um—want to go to my flat to check if there's anything in the mail from Justine—only I haven't... My car's not here.'

'I'll drive you, of course...'

'Oh no, I didn't mean that!' Ellena exclaimed hurriedly. 'What I was going to ask, was that, if you aren't using your car yourself, if I may borrow it.'

Gideon stared at her in dumbfounded surprise. 'Oh, my stars, Ellena,' he said after a moment. 'You slay me!'

'I knew I shouldn't have asked!'

'Yes, you should,' he replied. 'It's because of our—arrangement—that you're without your vehicle for the moment. And, while it's true I do have some work in my study that I could be getting on with, my housekeeper is looking on us all misty-eyed and I just haven't the heart to shatter her illusions by shutting myself away and depriving myself of your company.'

'Your charm's back,' Ellena commented faintly.

Gideon stared at her. For an age, it seemed to her, he just sat and stared at her. Then, 'Thank heavens for that,' he mocked, but was serious as he went on, 'How do you fancy incorporating your plans for the day with my plans for the day?' She had no idea what he meant, and looked at him as if trying to gauge what he intended.

'Give me a hint,' she suggested.

'How about first of all I show you my old nursery, followed by a trip to your flat, followed by a quick bite to eat somewhere, followed by a shopping spree for whatever you think is needed to modernise the nursery, ready for when we bring our niece home?'

'Oh, Gideon!' Ellena cried, and, her emotions wobbly of late, and touched by his thoughtfulness, she had a feeling she might break down in floods of tears at any moment. Which caused her to struggle desperately for something light to say. 'If I weren't married to you, I'd say you'd be quite a catch for somebody,' she managed.

Solemnly he stared back at her. 'You're not so bad yourself, Mrs Langford,' he replied—at which her fear of tears vanished and they both burst out laughing.

Half an hour later, they were inspecting the nursery quarters housed on the top floor. It consisted of a playroom, bedroom and kitchen and, like all the others in the house, the rooms were large, though empty of furniture. Ellena was glancing round the spotless bedroom, struck by its light and airy feel, when something else suddenly struck her.

'It's pink!' she exclaimed of the palest pink walls.

'True,' Gideon replied.

'You were all boys!'

'True,' he answered again.

'Your mother wanted a girl?'

'Probably. Although up until last Saturday the walls—and the furniture I moved out—were blue.'

Oh, Gideon! Was he special, or was he special? Feeling that the tears she had striven so hard not to shed might yet get the better of her, Ellena went and took a look out of the window. She swallowed hard. 'You've had it redecorated,' she said, and, turning, regained the control she needed. 'How long will it be, do you think, before we have Violette?' she asked.

'Soon,' Gideon promised. 'Trust me. Quite soon.'

She wanted him to be more specific, wanted to ask, how, why, and what was happening on the legal front. But, with the evidence before her, of the pale pink of the nursery, that Gideon had waited only to hear her say last Saturday that she would marry him before he'd straight away got the decorators in, she knew she could trust him. That 'quite soon' meant the first possible moment.

'In that case, it seems to me we'd better hurry and get some nursery furniture delivered as soon as we can.'

They delayed only for Gideon to show her the connecting self-contained apartment which the nanny would use, then they walked down to the landing below and to where their own bedrooms lay. His door came first; Ellena left him, and entered her own room.

She washed her hands and tidied her hair and, conscious the whole time of the open door between their two rooms, sorted through her wardrobe for the jacket she wanted.

'Ready?' Gideon strolled into her room. It seemed ridiculous to object.

'I'll just put my jacket on,' she answered evenly, and most oddly felt her insides go like jelly when he came over, took it from her and, after holding it up for her to put on, caught hold of her hair and pulled it out from her collar.

'Fascinating colour,' he commented. 'Blonde with streaks of gold. Is it natural?'

She took a few steps away from him, strangely still able to feel his fingers in her hair, warm against her neck. 'As a matter of fact, yes,' she answered. 'Though it's no wonder to me you know so much.' What he didn't know, he found out!

His lips twitched. 'Stop me if I ask too many questions,' he invited, and, going to her bedroom door, he opened it. They left by that route.

Ellena was in a very sober frame of mind when they pulled up outside her flat. 'I shouldn't be long, but if you'd like to come up for a minute or two…' she offered.

He didn't answer but accepted by going with her into the building and up to her flat. Disappointment awaited her. There was nothing in the post apart from a couple of circulars.

'I didn't really expect anything,' she murmured, looking away from him. Though she guessed she wasn't making a very good job of hiding from him how wretched she felt not to have an alive-and-well communication from her sister when, as she turned from him, Gideon caught a hold of her.

Like a homing pigeon she went into his arms. A moment of weakness it might have been but for a brief while she obeyed the instinct to lean her head against his chest. She felt safe, secure, comforted—yet at the same time she had a funny sort of feeling inside, to be held close by him, wrapped in his firm strong arms.

'They'll be all right,' Gideon said to the top of her head. And because she knew he was hurting too, she could do nothing else but put her arms around him. 'We have to believe that, Ellena,' he murmured gently, and placed a light kiss on her hair.

She looked up, straight into a pair of direct and steady slate-grey eyes. And suddenly her unhappiness started to recede and she felt she wanted him to kiss her, to kiss her mouth. And, as they gazed at each other, she thought for one crazy moment that he was going to.

She took her arms from him, took a step back, common sense clamouring for a hearing. 'A fine pair of guardians we are,' she found her voice out of a breathless nowhere.

He let go of her. 'One half of us is beautiful,' he said.

'You've been looking in your mirror again,' she mocked with a laugh. It was senseless that she felt instantly brighter because he thought her beautiful.

'Let's shop,' he decreed.

By mutual consent they decided it was too early for lunch, and that they would eat later. They shopped, and shopped—nothing was too good for the infant they hoped to soon have in their care. And yet, even while eating, drinking, playing and sleeping equipment began to mount up, Ellena found her thoughts returning again and again to that time at her flat earlier, to the haven of Gideon's arms, to the fact that she had wanted him to kiss her.

She and Justine had been on their own for so long now, and she'd had to be the one with the sensible head. So had it been purely that it was comforting to relax and let somebody else take charge for a change? But he wasn't taking charge, it was a joint thing. Grief, she'd been held by a man before, be it only in a warm-up embrace that had not gone much further—but she couldn't ever remember feeling this way before! What on earth was happening to her?

Nothing was happening to her, she decided very firmly. It was just that she was going through a very emotional time at the moment. Ellena tuned back in to the discussion Gideon was having with the salesman when she heard him say that he wanted the chest of drawers, the cot and its bedding, together with a whole host of other paraphernalia, delivered the next day.

'We're having Violette with us tomorrow?' Ellena asked him eagerly the first moment that they were alone.

'No,' Gideon straight away disabused her of that idea. 'I said soon, and I meant soon. I merely want to have the nursery ready to eliminate any "You haven't so much as a cot for her to sleep in'' argument, when the time comes.'

'Did I mention before your ability to think streets in advance of anyone else?'

'I think you've just paid me a compliment.'

'Don't let it go to your head. I meant nothing personal by it.'

'My dear,' Gideon drawled, 'we don't have that sort of a marriage.'

So put me in my place, why don't you! Ellena fumed, wishing she hadn't spoken and not liking the arrogant devil after all. She was only trying to be friendly. 'What's the latest from your lawyers?' she asked snappily.

Gideon looked surprised. 'You're a sensitive soul, aren't you?' he questioned.

'Don't tell me that you, with all your research, have never come across a type like me!' She took refuge from bruised feelings in sarcasm, though she was aware of Gideon's steady and considering gaze on her for long seconds before he answered.

'Do you know, Ellena, I rather think I haven't. I knew before there was something different about you. Now I realise that you are not merely different—you're unique.'

She had no idea how she was meant to take his remark, whether to be pleased or offended.

'I'm certainly not as clever as you,' she admitted. 'You can tell a compliment from a mile off—I don't know whether I've just been insulted or complimented.'

'Would I insult my wife?' he asked solemnly.

She had an idea he was laughing at her. 'So what's with the lawyers?' she insisted.

'They're put on ice, for the moment,' he deigned to answer. 'It will be natural, should the worst have happened, that you and I as next of kin take the baby. But, until we know that for sure, and if you're willing, I'd like to hold back from taking court action to have her legally declared ours.' He was talking about adoption! He was talking as if, were the worst to have happened, they would take steps to legally adopt Violette! Ellena, while not wanting to look too far into the future, could only think with all her heart of Violette's well being.

'I'm willing,' she confirmed, and wanted to add the proviso providing they *had* Violette living with them at some early date. But, as Gideon had reminded her, he had said she *would* soon be with them, and that meant soon. She didn't want him to think of her as some carping female—though why she should want his good opinion defeated her.

She didn't care a light for his opinion of her,
she decided promptly. Regardless of the facts
that they had shopped well into lunchtime, and
seemed to have bought up the store—their list
of requirements now completed—Ellena decided he could lunch on his own.

'Actually, it seems senseless for you to drive
me in on Monday when I'm near enough to my
flat to go and collect my car now,' she informed
him.

'You're proposing to drive home without
me?' Gideon queried, and Ellena felt quite
misty-eyed. How lovely that word 'home'
sounded. How lovely that Gideon should refer
to his house as her home. She took a steadying
breath—grief, was she as sensitive as he suggested?

'Anything wrong with that?'

'I know this is your first honeymoon, my
dear,' he drawled, 'and I know you've a definite
lack of experience in the togetherness depart-
ment, but have you considered, for a moment,
our housekeeper's romantic sensibilities?'

It was utterly crackers, to Ellena's mind, not
to pick up her car while she had the opportunity.
And yet, so much might rest on their being seen
together—on their supposedly being too much
in love to want to be parted. 'How could I bear

to be apart from you for so much as a moment?'
she offered.

'So we'll eat.'

It was a late lunch, but it was a pleasant affair. They discussed many things of a non-
personal nature, and that suited Ellena fine. She
had always thought of herself as having a fairly
even temperament, but, recalling how bruised
she'd felt when Gideon had referred to their impersonal marriage, she had no wish to invite the
bruised experience again.

Somehow, after that, the time simply flew.
They returned to the home they now shared and
when Ellena just could not resist going along to
the nursery to mentally place the furniture that
would be arriving tomorrow, she turned on a
sound—and found Gideon had followed and
was watching her.

'How did I know I'd find you here?' he
asked.

She smiled at him, unable to remember a time
when she hadn't liked him too well. 'I was just
deciding where everything would go. Er, with
your agreement,' she added hastily, lest he had
views on the subject.

'I'll leave that entirely up to you,' he answered, and came to the purpose of why he had
come looking for her. 'Mrs Morris wondered if

you had any special likes and dislikes for dinner?'

'Oh, heavens. I'm still full from lunch!' Ellena exclaimed, only then realising that, as mistress of Oakvale, she had the responsibility of discussing menus with their housekeeper. 'I'd better go and have a word with her,' she decided. 'Then I'm going to walk off our last meal.' She had seen little of the surrounding countryside yet. 'Um—talking of togetherness...' he wanted togetherness, she'd give him togetherness '...you'd better come with me.'

Gideon gave her a startled look, then good humour was spreading across his features. 'What have I married?' he asked, amused.

'A bossy woman. Come on.'

Ellena spent a pleasant ten minutes or so with Mrs Morris, and had an extremely pleasant walk with Gideon. After which she went up to her room and closed the communicating door. Then she took a leisurely bath and, while still extremely anxious underneath about Justine and Kit, she felt better than she had in a long while.

Dinner with Gideon was a relaxed affair. He had an uncanny knack, though, of drawing from her matters which, while not in any way secret, she had always felt were private.

'Did you always want to be an accountant?' he asked at one juncture—and Ellena found she was telling him of her university plans before her parents had died, and how fortunate she regarded herself that Andrea had given her the chance to train with her. 'She's been wonderful,' Ellena went on. 'Always very understanding when things with Justine got a bit fraught.'

'Justine was a tearaway?'

'Understatement!' Ellena smiled.

'Out all hours?'

'That doesn't make her a wicked person!'

'Put your hackles down. We've already agreed that she and Kit are a pair well met.'

'Sorry,' she apologised, and Gideon smiled at her across the table.

'So, in between keeping an eye on her—which probably meant charging around in the middle of the night looking for her—and studying for your accountancy exams, you never had any time to get your own social life going.'

'Oh, it wasn't that bad!' she denied, not liking the idea that this man should think her as green as grass, never had a boyfriend, a dullard. 'I've had my moments too.'

'Boyfriends?'

'Of course.'

'Anyone special?'

Ellena shook her head, and, though it went against the grain, felt compelled to confess, 'I never went out with anyone long enough to find out.'

'A half a dozen times?' he suggested.

'More like two,' she had to admit. 'Then some crisis with Justine would crop up and I'd have to cancel. With Justine going from crisis to crisis I got fed up with breaking dates and decided I'd rather concentrate on my studies and her.'

'With Justine always coming first?'

'What can I tell you?' He had a brother she rather thought he'd drop everything for. 'But my sister wasn't always giving me headaches,' Ellena went on quickly. 'She was wild, certainly. Impetuous, unthinking, reckless—a living nightmare sometimes—those words all apply. But she was warm, loving, funny—and as honest as the day.' She paused, a most unpalatable truth she had never been able to shrug off getting to her again.

'What is it?' Gideon asked urgently. 'There's such pain in your eyes.'

'I'm sorry,' she apologised. 'I've tried telling myself that Justine's hormones must be still all over the place after having Violette, and they've caused her to act in a way totally alien to her.

But she's so honest; I just know she wouldn't dream of flitting from a hotel without settling her account first. She just *wouldn't*—I *know* her!'

Gideon considered what she had said for a moment then, hormones aside, came up with another explanation. 'She may have thought Kit had settled the account.'

Ellena wanted to believe that. Not to believe it would mean that Justine and Kit had not left their hotel. That they had gone out that morning of the avalanche intending to return—only something had prevented them from returning. 'Justine was the one with the money,' she reminded him shakily.

Gideon had not forgotten but he was, it seemed, determined not to lose heart. 'If she's anywhere near as sensitive as her sister, I'd say she handed over some money rather than let Kit feel small.'

There had been plenty of time in which Justine could have used one of her credit cards to obtain some local currency, Ellena saw, currency which, without a doubt, she would most certainly have shared with Kit. But even while Ellena was musing on that, her heartbeat seemed to quicken at the gentle way Gideon was looking at her.

Abruptly, she changed the subject. 'So—um—how about you?' she questioned, striving hard for a bright note.

'Me?' he queried.

'I've told you all about my love-life, and, given I've only skated on its perimeters, fair's fair.'

'You're suggesting I tell you of my love-life?'

'Well, you needn't go into too many details,' she qualified hastily.

He laughed. She liked him. But then he shook his head. 'That,' he said sadly, 'I cannot do.'

She knew that she didn't want him to, but some devil was pushing her. 'Why not?' she insisted.

'It's the code,' he answered; his laughter was gone but his eyes were amused.

'What code?'

He looked at her. Looked at her as if he enjoyed doing so. Somehow, when her heart had started to jig about a bit, Ellena had managed to hold his gaze. 'Men—don't,' he informed her.

'Hound!' They both smiled.

Ellena lay in her bed that night giving herself a talking to. She owned that Gideon Langford was getting to her, that she found him stimulating, and that she enjoyed being in his company.

But it would never do. He was entertaining her, was having her live in his home, indeed had gone so far as to marry her—purely as a smokescreen. But there was nothing personal in it—not that she wanted there to be, for goodness' sake—but it wouldn't hurt to remember that. It was just that it was in their mutual interests to be seen together. Ellena went to sleep that night, with the view that while she would play her part in this togetherness thing when anyone else was around, at other times she was going to keep out of Gideon's way. In the interests of self-preservation... Abruptly Ellena doubled back on her drowsy thoughts. Self-preservation? Gosh, she must be more tired than she had thought. What did she need self-preservation for?

She found she had no trouble in keeping out of Gideon's way over the next couple of days, however, for, regardless of Mrs Morris's romantic sensibilities, he seemed hardly ever to be around.

'You can borrow my car if you wish,' he offered at breakfast time the next morning.

Somehow that annoyed her. He could keep his magnanimous gestures! 'Thanks all the same, I hadn't planned to go anywhere today apart from the nursery.'

'Give me a shout when the furniture arrives—I'll be in my study.'

Ellena looked at him. She had an idea he had gone off her. Well, she wasn't so keen on him just then, either. 'I'll do that,' she answered coolly, and received a cool stare back—and that was about the sum total of their conversation.

She did not have to tell him when the furniture arrived. He heard the vehicle pull up. They had done well yesterday, she realised, when a pretty chest of drawers was carted into the nursery, followed by a cot and a padded highchair.

Gideon returned to the nursery once he'd seen the delivery men on their way. She again wanted to ask him *when*, but just then realised that she trusted him, and knew that when he said 'soon', no man would do it sooner.

'I don't remember you buying that!' he said when he saw the pretty smocked dress she was taking out of its tissue, ready to place it in the chest of drawers, once she'd given them a wipe out.

'You'll have to be quicker than that,' she returned lightly, and saw that it looked as if he was striving hard not to let his lips twitch.

He did not smile. In fact the rest of that day, and the whole of Sunday, seemed to be designated No Smiling Days.

Ellena was glad when Monday came around. She heard Gideon moving about very early and leapt out of bed and headed for the shower. He was giving her a lift in; it would be a fine start to the week if she kept him waiting!

As she had assumed, they left the house far earlier than she had planned to once she had her own wheels. They passed the journey in relative silence. But, on arriving at her flat, ever mindful of photographers, even though Ellena thought it most improbable that one of them would be stationed at her address, Gideon got out of the car and came to stand on the pavement with her.

She looked up at him, unsure about what happened now. He looked down, pinning her with those steady slate-grey eyes. 'Enjoy your day,' he bade her.

'You too,' she answered politely, and felt instantly all hot and bothered when he bent down and kissed her on the mouth.

She turned away. Perhaps, if they were still together in a month's time, his kisses would have been relegated to her cheeks. You're growing cynical, Ellena, go and get your car.

She was extremely busy at work that day, and she was glad it was so. Still, all the same, there were many times when Justine came into her head and, most unexpectedly, and many times, thoughts of the man she had married would arrive unbidden too—and require quite some moving.

Everyone at the office was most kind and, to her huge embarrassment, which she hoped she covered well, they had made a collection and presented her with a most beautiful cut-glass vase. There was also a bouquet of flowers to go with it.

Oh, what a sham it all was! A very necessary sham, she quieted her conscience a moment later. She wanted Violette. She was not, not, not going to leave her with that dreadful woman! And, having married in order to claim her, then if she had to be *happily* married, there'd be none happier.

She thanked everyone sincerely and escaped back to her office. She had only another unexpected hiccup to her day when one of Andrea's best clients came in to see her at the close of business, upset that, because he hadn't an appointment, Andrea was tied up and had passed him on to Ellena.

'It was only a small piece of advice I wanted,' Cliff Wilkinson protested. 'And you know how difficult it is for me to come and see her in normal office hours.'

'I know it isn't easy,' Ellena sympathised, aware that Cliff, who was nice, not bad looking and thirty-eight to Andrea's forty-two, was en-amoured of her employer and had most probably called this late hoping to extend a business dis-cussion into dinner. It had happened before, only Andrea, who didn't want to know, had in-vited Ellena along, as part of her training, to be an unwanted third guest. 'I'm sure that I can—' Ellena broke off—Cliff had spotted her bouquet.

'It's your birthday?' he guessed.

Oh, crumbs. She'd rather keep quiet. But any girl who'd married only last Thursday would, she felt sure, be keen to announce it from the rooftops. 'I—um—got married last week,' she revealed, feeling herself growing pink.

Cliff, like the nice person he was, forgot his disappointment that Andrea wasn't available to see him, and showed only delight at her news. 'Congratulations!' he exclaimed enthusiasti-cally. 'Though it's your husband I should be congratulating.'

'Thank you,' she murmured, desperately wanting to change the subject, while at the same time wanting to play her role to perfection.

'I'm keeping you!' Cliff suddenly realised. 'You'll want to get off home. Of course you do.'

He stood up. 'Perhaps you'll tell Mrs Keyte that I'll come back another day.'

Ellena protested that she'd be pleased to advise him on his problem but he wouldn't hear of it. And, since she guessed it was more a problem he had invented so he could have a one-to-one with Andrea, Ellena did not press it.

She was delayed leaving the office and took some papers with her in her briefcase. But, late though she was, she drove first to her flat. The mail normally arrived some while after she had set out for work. There had been nothing there for her this morning; there was nothing there for her now. But she refused to be down-hearted and moved about her flat, wondering if she should make herself something to eat there, or go to her other home.

It was the thought that Mrs Morris might possibly be offended if she had gone to the trouble to prepare something for her that decided Ellena. This and her togetherness pact with Gideon Langford.

Her phone rang; she quickly answered it. 'Hello?' she said—talk of the devil!

'Do you intend coming home tonight?' Gideon questioned aggressively.

Who *did* he think he was? 'How could I stay away?' she answered sweetly—and put down the phone.

Ratfink! Perversely, she wanted to stay away another hour. However, thoughts of offending Mrs Morris neutralised her feelings.

Ellena drove to the home she now shared with Gideon—albeit temporarily—realising that he must have left his office early. Strange! Somehow she'd thought, without actually being aware of thinking it, in normal times he'd probably be the last one to leave the office.

A smile of merriment lit her mouth. No doubt he couldn't wait to get home that day. Togetherness; he couldn't possibly wait another moment to rush home to his bride. What a pity his bride wasn't there!

Ellena pulled up on the drive of Oakvale and, with no idea if there was anywhere special she had to garage her car, she paused only to pick up her briefcase, floral bouquet, shoulder bag and crystal vase, and left her vehicle where it was.

The front door opened before she rang the bell. Gideon stood there, tall, straight, sort of impatient—her heart started pounding a little erratically.

'Glad to see you. I'm laden.' She ignored her wayward emotions.

Gideon relieved her of her briefcase and stood back for her to enter. 'What's with the flowers?' he gritted when he saw the presentation bouquet.

'A present,' she said, and would have added an acid 'from an admirer', only just then she spotted Mrs Morris hovering in the hall. 'They made a collection at the office...' Her voice tailed off when, without more ado, Gideon took the flowers and the cut-glass vase from her hands and passed them over to his housekeeper.

'I've a present for you too,' he announced solemnly. 'At a guess, I'd say a ten to fourteen pound one.' And, while Ellena stared at him uncomprehending, 'It's waiting for you...' he broke off, his slate-grey eyes on hers '...up in the nursery.'

Ellena stared at him, caught Mrs Morris's beaming smile and—click! Her bag went down, and Ellena was haring up the stairs, up to the top floor. Along the landing she ran. She opened the nursery door.

A matronly woman with a wonderful homely face was standing in the nursery. In her arms, she held a baby. 'Violette!' Ellena cried huskily and, hurrying forward, took the baby from her.

How long she held the little scrap to her, crooning, cuddling, loving, she had no idea. But suddenly she became aware that Gideon was in the room too. She took her attention from the baby, and, her heart full, she said chokily, 'Thank you, Gideon. Oh, thank you.'

For long, silent moments he stared back at her, then he answered quietly, 'For you, my dear, anything.'

CHAPTER FIVE

SO MANY questions rushed to Ellena's lips as she looked from the baby to Gideon. Discretion ruled the day. Later, perhaps at dinner when they were alone, she would have the opportunity to ask him how he had performed the miracle of wresting Violette from that avaricious woman, who had never looked like giving her up.

'For you, my dear, anything,' he'd said. Ellena knew he had only said it because there was another person there with them, and that they must still maintain a loving front. But, most peculiarly, in this happiest of moments, she felt she would not have minded had he truly meant it.

She gave her undivided attention to being re-united with her niece and learned that Marjorie Dale, the woman who had temporary charge of the nursery, had everything under control. Although Mrs Dale had her own home in the village, she would be sleeping at Oakvale that night in a next-door bedroom that was to be turned into a bed-sitting room.

147

Ellena wanted to protest that there was no need for Mrs Dale to sleep over, that she would use that room and be on hand should Violette not sleep through until morning. She held back. Gideon must have a lot to tell her; she would wait to hear it all before she made any decisions regarding her niece's care.

Meantime, when Gideon had disappeared, she cuddled and loved the baby some more, and only reluctantly gave her up when Gideon returned. 'Mrs Morris delayed dinner for you,' he hinted, and Ellena was torn between wanting to stay right where she was, yet at the same time wanting to put a half-dozen or more questions to Gideon—namely why hadn't he let her know Violette was there sooner. Reluctantly, she handed the baby over to Marjorie Dale.

'Have you eaten?' she thought to ask her.

'Yes, thank you, Mrs Langford,' the woman replied.

Ellena left the nursery. She felt awkward. Mrs Langford! Ellena Langford! Ellena Spencer Langford! Crikey! Suddenly she realised that Gideon was right there beside her. 'I'll just slip off and wash my hands,' she murmured when they reached the next landing. She halted momentarily, expecting him to go down the stairs. He didn't, but stood looking at her.

Earlier that day she had drawn her gold spun blonde hair back from her face in a classic knot. She looked down at the dark trouser suit and white shirt she had worn all day. 'I won't change,' she told him, for no reason other than she thought she had kept Mrs Morris waiting long enough.

'It's amazing,' he answered.

He was still looking at her—she was lost to his meaning. 'What is?'

'That you've reached the age of twenty-two without some man making off with you.'

'You're saying I look all right?' Where had that imp of mischief come from?

'You're beautiful and you know it.'

'You can't blame a girl for fishing,' she grinned, and went on her way.

A quick wash of her hands later and she was heading down the stairs, wondering at this light-heartedness that had overtaken her. Was it purely because of the fact that Justine's daughter was now under the same roof? It couldn't be because, in contrast to the last two days, Gideon suddenly seemed light-hearted too, could it?

He was standing talking to Mrs Morris when she entered the dining room. 'I'm sorry to have kept you waiting,' Ellena apologised, unsure as to which of them she was apologising to.

Gideon pulled out her chair and Mrs Morris went on her way, looking every bit as if, in this instance of their new arrival, it didn't matter a scrap how long she had to delay dinner. Ellena had an idea that Violette Ellena Langford might end up being one very spoilt young lady.

'So?' she questioned, the moment she and Gideon sat down at the table. 'You obviously phoned me at my flat to tell me that you'd managed to bring Violette home.' His aggressively phrased, 'Do you intend coming home tonight?', had told her precisely nothing. But now there were more important matters to discuss here. 'So tell me, how, why, where?' she asked.

'You're pleased, obviously.'

'Never more so,' she replied. 'You said "soon" and I've kept hoping, but didn't like to keep asking in case you thought I was a nag.'

'That bothered you?' he questioned, an eyebrow going aloft.

Why had it bothered her that he might think her carping? She couldn't find an answer. 'Are you being annoying on purpose?' she questioned shortly.

His lips twitched. 'So, to start at the beginning. I rang Russell after our wedding last Thursday to apologise for not inviting him and his lady to it, and to tell him I wanted him to know before he read it in the papers the next day.'

Ellena remembered the press photographers at the registry office. 'Was he upset?' He was family after all. 'That you hadn't invited him?'

'He lives in his own world,' Gideon stated. 'But, while I felt pretty certain he'd remember to tell his wife that you and I were married—' more the object of the telephone call, Ellena realised '—I had a pleasant surprise when he told me they wouldn't have been able to come anyway because their nanny had walked out. In between coping with the incessant crying of an upset infant, Pamela had spent the day on the phone endeavouring to find a replacement nanny.'

'You should have told me!' was Ellena's first reaction.

'What—so you could be upset too?' he countered. Had he not told her of the nanny's departure because he'd thought better than to cause her upset over something she could do little about? He had called her sensitive—Ellena was beginning to think that Gideon was also far more sensitive than she had credited. 'I knew it would worry you,' he went on, 'but it seemed to me that the more exacting the little one became, the sooner my sister-in-law would have enough of her.'

'Was she unable to hire another nanny?'

'Hiring a nanny wasn't the problem. Getting one to stay was another matter. I rang Russell this morning to enquire how things were with the baby. Nanny number two had just walked out and Pamela was going up the wall. Time, I felt, to pay her a visit.'

'She handed Violette over just like that?' Ellena, remembering the hard-faced woman, could barely believe it.

'She put up a small show of resistance, but against our marriage certificate, her non-maternal instincts and her inability to cope with a fractious four-and-a-half-month-old, she folded when money changed hands.'

'You paid her!'

'I always knew I was going to have to—it was just a matter of timing. We had to be married—it would be a bonus if, as turned out, her nerves were frazzled.'

'I've said it before—you're clever, aren't you?'

'I like to think I've got everything covered,' he replied mock-modestly.

Her lips twitched. She concentrated on the matter in hand. 'You brought Violette back with you there and then?'

'I'd taken the precaution of calling on Marjorie Dale in the village first.'

'You took her with you?' she asked amazed.

'I thought of you, firstly, but felt it would be too distressing for you if the little one was still wailing and Pamela wouldn't hand her over. So I fitted the car baby seat you'd left in the nursery and took Marjorie Dale, hoping she'd be necessary—nothing would be lost if she wasn't,' he answered. 'Marjorie has always helped out here in one capacity or another. She's a widow with children at university. Apparently, as well as having majored in common sense, Marjorie positively adores babies.' His lips most definitely did twitch when he added, 'I thought her a most likely candidate to pass muster under your exacting requirements.'

'You make me sound like an ogre!'

'Not at all. I'm just aware of how very seriously you take your responsibilities to that little lady upstairs. Marjorie and the new qualified nanny who arrives tomorrow will between them ensure that our niece lacks for neither love nor attention.'

'Just a second!' he was racing on too fast! New nanny! Looking after Violette between them? 'When did the new nanny come in?'

'Didn't I say?' He knew darn well he hadn't! 'There was just time when we got back for me to interview Beverly Clark, most highly spoken of by the agency. She liked us, cooed over the infant, and passed the inspections by both Mrs Morris and Marjorie Dale. If you don't take to her, though,' he inserted, 'then we'll find somebody else.'

Ellena had started to grow a little annoyed that all this had taken place without him consulting her. But, in view of him being prepared to let Beverly Clark go if she wasn't happy about her, Ellena didn't think she could raise too much of an objection. 'You know that I intend to look after Violette myself at the weekends.'

'If that's what you want, you still can. But you do an exacting job too, remember. You may be glad to be able to hand her to someone else while you take a break. I believe tots like that can sometimes grizzle on endlessly with no cause whatsoever.'

All the time they'd been talking, they had been eating. Neither of them had bothered with a first course, and Ellena had a few minutes to think over everything that had been said when

Mrs Morris came in and cleared their main course dishes. They were both having cheese and biscuits to finish.

'You've got everything worked out, by the look of it,' Ellena commented, once Mrs Morris had gone from the dining room.

'You don't sound very happy about it?'

'I should have liked to be consulted,' Ellena stated, but tacked on, as in all honesty she must, 'Though it's a fact I don't think I could have improved on anything you've done.'

Gideon looked at her for quite some moments, then, his eyes roving her dainty features, her perfect skin and her eyes, he stated quietly, 'You're so honest. Beautiful on the inside, as well as out.'

She blushed, she knew she did. She wanted to say something witty, something clever, sharp. But her wits seemed to have deserted her, and what she did say was a quiet, husky, 'Thank you.' But this would never do, and to counteract the sudden banging of her heart for no reason against her ribs, she asked politely, 'Do we get divorced now?'

His eyes were still on her, his look growing incredulous. 'My stars—you really are something else again!' he grunted. And if she wanted a blunt answer she soon had it, when he curtly told her, 'No, we do not get divorced now!'

'Pardon me for asking!' she snapped, and, refusing to be intimidated, she asked belligerently, 'Why not?'

'We haven't been married a week yet!' he retorted.

As if that was the end of the subject! 'What's that got to do with anything?' Ellena tossed back.

She had the heat drawn from her anger when, as they sat glaring at each other, Gideon's lips suddenly started to twitch. 'I'm enjoying the—rest—for one thing,' he drawled, and, while her sense of humour stirred at his reference to his having a break from his women friends—and all *that* entailed!—Ellena felt confusion, too, when she found herself staring at his mouth. He really had quite a divine sort of mouth. Grief! Rapidly she forced her glance away and saw he had been watching her. She refused to colour up again when, with those slate-grey eyes piercing hers, he went on, 'For another thing, in my view my sister-in-law gave in too easily. I don't trust her.'

'You think she'll try and get Violette back?' Ellena no longer felt amused.

'Give her a couple of days to get over the trauma of coping with a fretful infant and intractable nannies, and she'll be setting her devious mind to find some loophole.'

'You think she'll challenge you in court—even though you have—er—recompensed her!' Ellena gasped.

'That one has pound sterling signs stamped on her eyeballs—she'll try.'

'But she won't win?'

'Who could—against the two of us?'

'United we stand...' Ellena didn't finish, nor did she wish to consider a divorce any further. 'We stay married,' she agreed. She had eaten all she wanted. She got to her feet. 'I've a little work to do; I'll go up,' she said.

Gideon was on his feet too. 'I can put another desk in my study,' he offered.

'Now, isn't that kind!' Ellena replied in sincere amazement. 'But I shouldn't dream of disturbing you,' she declined. And added promptly, 'Goodnight, Gideon.'

She left him and went up the stairs. At their head she halted. Then, for all she guessed her niece must be asleep, she could not resist going up the extra flight to take a look at her.

Violette was safe, gorgeous and cherubic in sleep. Ellena whispered a goodnight to Marjorie

Dale and returned to her own room to find that, from the evidence of her briefcase on her bed, Gideon had been to her room. A smile lit her face—with so much else happening, she had forgotten he had taken it from her when she had arrived home earlier.

She had meant to thank him the next morning but passed him in the hall on his way out to an early meeting when she went down to breakfast. True, she was delayed—she'd popped up to the nursery.

'Bye, my dear,' he said, and, putting an arm around her, he kissed her.

She didn't move. His kiss was for the benefit of Mrs Morris, who must be about. Ellena realised that even as she acknowledged that his kiss seemed to be a little longer than the others he had bestowed on her.

'Er—bye,' she answered, and, grateful that he knew nothing about the nonsense going on inside her, she watched him stride purposefully to the door.

When she did move and turn, Ellena saw no sign of the housekeeper, but knew without a doubt that sharp-eyed Gideon must have spotted her as she had gone from the kitchen to the breakfast room.

Ellena had her breakfast and, running a little late, dashed upstairs to collect her jacket and briefcase from her bedroom, and—by the skin of her teeth—remembered to open the communicating door wide. Gideon, she saw, had remembered to dent the other pillow.

A fortnight later, and opening the door between the two rooms had become a habit. As, too, a visit to the nursery each morning was a must. Beverly Clark was a super nanny, and Ellena knew she could not have chosen better herself. Beverly was a stocky, sensible female of around twenty-four, dedicated to her work and perfectly matched to work with Marjorie Dale. The two got on famously—but were pleased to allow Ellena some time with her niece.

So, on that front, Ellena could not have been more happy. But the day when Justine and Kit should have returned came and went, causing her more than a little anxiety. Gideon had been again to Kit's flat and had left a note for Kit to contact him immediately and most urgently on his return, but so far had heard nothing.

Ellena still returned to her own flat first thing every evening to check her mail, but there was never anything from her sister. She refused to give up hope and put all her energies into the knowledge that, if the fancy took Justine, she was as likely to stay away for three or four months as the month or so she had stated.

After her usual, disappointing mail-checking visit to her flat that Tuesday evening, Ellena drove home to Oakvale in a grave frame of mind. Gideon had mentioned at breakfast that he had a business dinner to attend that evening and would be late home; his only reason for telling her was, she well knew, so that she wouldn't look surprised should the housekeeper refer to it in any way.

Ellena left her briefcase on the landing when she went up to the nursery. 'How's this bundle of joy been today?' she asked Beverly, as the nanny placed the thriving mite into her arms.

'She has her moments, but, for the most part, she's a little gem,' Beverly replied, clearly won over by her young charge.

As was Mrs Morris, Ellena learned when she later went down to eat her solitary meal, for the housekeeper seemed to have only one topic of conversation these days, and that was the baby.

Most evenings Ellena spent some time in the nursery, playing with the baby, or helping out when there was anything left to do. If Violette was sleepy, and also for the way it looked, she would sometimes go back down to the drawing room, occasionally spending some time chatting to Gideon after dinner if he was around.

But that evening he wasn't there and after her meal Ellena experienced such a feeling of restlessness, of being unable to settle, that she returned upstairs. She paid a visit to the nursery, but Violette was asleep, and, not wanting to intrude on Beverly's time off, Ellena returned to her room.

She had some complicated corporation accounts in her briefcase, something she normally enjoyed, but she couldn't settle to that either. She got the work out anyway, and laid it on the medium-sized antique desk which had magically appeared in her room when she'd arrived home two weeks ago. Gideon, of course.

Her thoughts stayed with him, this man she had married—and would sooner or later divorce. He was excellent company. She wasn't missing him, was she? Was that why she was feeling so unsettled? What rot! For crying out loud, she rarely saw him, apart from at breakfast—and not always then. She went and closed the communicating door, remembering how twice last week he'd had early appointments, and had been off and away before she'd gone down the stairs. She saw him most evenings, though, at dinner. But he, like her, brought work home, and would more often than not take himself off to his study.

Ellena was still avoiding her desk like the plague a half-hour later. It was ridiculous—she owned it was—but something *was* unsettling her. In an attempt to get more relaxed she went and had a bath and changed into a nonsense of a nightdress Justine had given her last Christmas, and then donned the matching silk wrap.

Fifteen minutes later, and she was thoroughly into the work on her desk. She was deep into facts and figures when, having lost count of time, she was suddenly aware of the communicating door opening.

Her eyes widened as Gideon entered her room. Her mouth went dry. He was fully dressed—she wasn't! 'I didn't hear you knock.' She said the first thing that came into her head.

He looked tired, she thought. He smiled; it took his look of tiredness away. 'I'm afraid I more lightly rapped than knocked.' He clearly hadn't wanted the rest of the house to hear that he had to hammer on his wife's bedroom door to be let in. 'You were obviously absorbed and didn't hear.' He came over to where she was sitting and looked over her shoulder. 'Looks complicated,' he commented of her paperwork.

'It took me five years to get the hang of it,' she quipped, referring to her long apprenticeship. Unconsciously, she arched her neck, pulling her shoulders back to release the tension of sitting in one position for an age.

'Here, let me,' Gideon offered—and, before she could stop him, his long, sensitive fingers were massaging her neck and shoulders.

'I…' she went to protest, but his hands were marvellous. Wonderful wasn't stretching it! 'Oh!' she exclaimed softly, the warmth of his touch suddenly starting to make a muddle of her. She never wanted him to stop. She closed her eyes. She was being seduced—and she was enjoying it. 'That was good,' she attempted to end it when she felt she could speak without sounding husky. Her voice *was* husky.

She turned in her chair; his hands fell away. Her warm blue eyes met warm slate-grey ones. She had a dreadful notion that he knew how she was feeling. 'Don't strain your lovely eyes burning the midnight oil,' he remarked evenly.

'I'm nearly through,' she managed. 'Er—did you have a good dinner?' She was making conversation near midnight and in her nightie! Brain! Where's your brain, girl?

'Fair,' he answered. 'We got caught up in heavy business discussions afterwards.'

'Naturally,' she smiled.

His eyes fell to her lips. He seemed to lean forward. It was all in her imagination, she realised, because as she quickly veiled her eyes, she thought, ooh, he was going to kiss her, and just then she didn't seem to have the strength to tell him she was more interested in her calculator than his kisses! Instead Gideon ambled over to the door through which he had just come in. 'In line with our togetherness policy, of letting one half know what the other half is doing, I've a very early appointment tomorrow and will be on my way before you're down to breakfast.'

'Thanks very much for letting me know,' Ellena smiled; there was nothing wrong with her manners. She wished she could say the same about the female he had just awakened in her who, with very small encouragement from him, was feeling extremely wayward—not to say wanton!

It took her a long time to get to sleep that night, and when she awakened the next morning she was still feeling restless. She had a moment's respite when she went up to the nursery and observed again how her niece was positively blossoming under the devoted care she was receiving.

That feeling of being unsettled was back with her again when she sat eating a brief but solitary breakfast. In a way she was glad that Gideon had left early. Somehow, and she could still feel the intimate warm touch of his hands through the thin silk of her covering, she was still feeling very much confused by the way she had wanted him to continue to massage, caress... Oh, grief. She closed her mind to such thoughts and went to work.

It was useless to run away, though, she discovered. For around mid-morning Andrea came to see her and said Cliff Wilkinson had been on the phone saying he'd be in town in the early evening, and would she meet him for dinner when they could discuss a problem he was having.

'Oh, dear,' Ellena sympathised, aware Andrea had been badly hurt in her marriage and was just not interested in giving any other man a chance.

'Precisely! I shall have to go—I can't get out of this one,' Andrea said, plainly trying to keep her personal feelings separate from business. 'But I've told him, since his problem seems to be quite involved, that I would bring an associate along.'

'He didn't like that?' Ellena guessed.

'He huffed and puffed. But in the end he agreed—provided it's you I bring with me. I know that, technically speaking, you're still on your honeymoon—which, of course, if I read the man correctly, is why he specifically stated you and no one else...'

'Clearly thinking that there was no way I'd want to miss dinner with my husband.' Ellena put in, and, smiling, added, 'I'd be delighted to prove Mr Wilkinson wrong.'

'I'll make it up to you,' Andrea promised gratefully.

'No need,' Ellena assured her, and when Andrea had left knew that because of their togetherness she should ring Gideon and let him know she would be late home. But then she recalled his touch, the way she had felt—and she was confused again.

Good manners were prodding at her, though, so that in the end she dialled Oakvale and spoke with Mrs Morris, explaining that she would not be at dinner, and asked her to mention it to Mr Langford.

'I couldn't get him at his office or on his mobile,' she perjured her soul, then heard that Violette had given the housekeeper the most gorgeous smile when Mrs Morris popped into the nursery "just for a minute", and felt warmed at yet another indication that everyone was spoiling Violette dreadfully.

Having covered herself for dinner, however, Ellena found that thoughts of Gideon constantly came between her and her work that day. So much so, that she found she was running late.

It had been her intention to drive to her flat, check her post and from there drive to the smart hotel where Cliff Wilkinson was staying for their seven o'clock dinner appointment.

That was the first of her plans which went wrong. It was an easy adjustment, though, to decide to pay a visit to her flat after dinner rather than before. Ellena was still at her desk at six when Andrea, who wasn't going home first either, came into her office looking green.

'Migraine,' she said faintly.

Ellena got her to the couch in the restroom, but could see that her boss was going nowhere but to her bed. 'I'll ring Cliff and cancel, then I'll drive you home,' Ellena took charge.

Only she found that, for all she was looking and feeling ghastly, Andrea was still able to make decisions. 'Don't cancel. He's important,' she decided.

Ellena didn't want to cause her any more hassle. 'I'll ring and tell him I'll be delayed,' she agreed soothingly. 'I'll take you home and...'

But Andrea had worked long and hard to get her business off the ground, and although in Ellena's book there was not the remotest chance that Cliff Wilkinson would go to another accountancy firm, Andrea stated the situation as she saw it. 'He's going to be offended that I'm not there—I'm not having him finishing with us because my representative turns up late.'

'You're not fit to drive!' Ellena argued.

'I couldn't if I tried!' Andrea agreed, going on to say she'd had these attacks before, she'd taken medication, and that a lie-down with the lights out for an hour or so would work wonders. 'By the time you're thinking of having coffee, I'll be home and in bed,' she assured her.

Contrary to her employer's opinion that Cliff Wilkinson would be offended that she wasn't there, once Ellena had assured him over dinner how genuine Andrea's migraine was, Cliff was more concerned than anything else.

'You say she's still at the office?'

'She should be coming out of it by now.'

'I'll go and see if she'll let me drive her home,' he promptly stated, and would have been off like a shot had Ellena not been able to convince him that what Andrea needed just then was utter quiet and darkness.

'She's promised me that in the event this attack doesn't soon clear, she'll call a taxi,' Ellena assured him—and was still assuring him when their first course arrived.

It took until the main course for them to get down to business, and Ellena became engrossed in his plan to extend some of his development to the London area.

By the pudding stage they were deep into discussion, with Ellena pointing out a financial aspect which, for all his business acumen, Cliff hadn't seemed to have thought of. 'Now I know why I need accountants,' he smiled, and Ellena smiled back—but, on glancing away, she looked up—staggeringly—straight into a pair of slate-grey eyes!

At that moment she felt that her heart would stop. Gideon! What was he doing here? There was, however, no time for her to think further. Goodness, he was looking furious about something! And, oh, help, he was coming over to their table!

Ellena had lost track completely of what Cliff Wilkinson was saying, and stared mesmerised as Gideon, not interested in being introduced, apparently, stopped at their table and, his pleasant tone much at variance with the hostility she saw in his steel-grey scrutiny, smiled. 'Hello, darling,' he greeted her, going on smoothly, 'Sorry I missed you at breakfast. I've something on, so can't stay, but I'll see you at home later.' With that, and without the smallest acknowledgment to her dinner partner, he turned abruptly about—and was gone.

Ellena was still feeling floored when she became aware that Cliff had just said something. She stared at him. 'Was that your husband?' he asked, and Ellena rapidly came to.

'I'm sorry. I would have introduced you, only…'

'Only he was in something of a hurry,' Cliff said soothingly.

Ellena didn't want soothing. Having got her second wind, she was starting to get angry. She hadn't misunderstood the hostility in Gideon's eyes, she knew she hadn't, nor his fury either. Who did he think he was? Did he think *he* was the only one allowed business dinners?

'I shouldn't have insisted that you come,' Cliff was going on.

Oh, grief, he was starting to sound guilty. 'Yes, you should. And I'm very happy to be of assistance,' she smiled. But she started to have some very dark thoughts about Gideon Langford, husband and swine!

'And I've enjoyed your company,' Cliff replied handsomely. 'But now I think I've taken up enough of your time. You must be longing to get back to your home and new husband.'

She'd trained for five years for this! To be sent home because she had some 'loving' man in the background. Like hell she'd go home! But their business was as near complete as made no difference. So she smiled and chatted—and hoped to see Gideon Langford on her way crossing the foyer, so she could give him a swift, hard kick on the shins. However, of the man she had married there was no sign.

Outside the hotel Cliff Wilkinson escorted her to her car. 'Thank you for a very pleasant dinner,' Ellena said, shaking hands with him. 'If you need to know anything further, I'll be very pleased to help.'

By the time she arrived at her flat, Cliff Wilkinson was long gone from her mind. What right had Gideon Langford to be mad at her? She'd done nothing wrong!

Her spirits dipped when she saw there was nothing in her post from Justine—but she refused to lose heart. She turned her thoughts on Andrea and wondered about phoning her. If her medication was working, though, she could be tucked up in bed and fast asleep. Ellena decided against it—and Gideon Langford, never absent for long, was back in her mind.

How dared he? She gave quite some angry thought to staying the night at her flat, and was still angry when she decided against it. Apart from anything else, should Pamela Langford have her scouts about, there was still their to-getherness to consider.

It was approaching midnight when, having worked herself up into a fine state, Ellena pulled up at Oakvale. Who did he think he was? she fumed again as she quietly entered the house. For all his smiling mouth, it was a slur on her professionalism to have him stand there glaring at her while she was dining with a client.

She climbed the stairs and went silently along the landing to her room. She wasn't having it; she wasn't! She shrugged out of her suit jacket, going to her wardrobe for a hanger. First thing tomorrow, at breakfast, she would tell Mr Furious-for-no-reason-Langford where he got off.

She hung up her jacket. First thing tomorrow she'd... She heard the sound of a door open-ing—she swung round! She wasn't going to have to wait until tomorrow! Framed in the open communicating door, Gideon stood there. Being furious, if his expression was anything to go by, was not her sole right.

She attempted to get in first, but he beat her to it. 'Where the hell have you been?' he demanded.

He wasn't wearing a watch. In fact, if his bare legs and what she could see of his bare chest were anything to go by, he wasn't wearing anything at all very much underneath the black towelling robe he had on.

'You know where I've been!' she snapped, dragging her eyes from the dark exposed hair on his chest.

'Till this hour?' he snarled aggressively, coming away from the doorway and further into her room.

She nearly reminded him that she was twenty-two, not sixteen, but she fell back on sarcasm instead. 'What happened to ''Hello, darling''?' What in creation had *he* got to be mad about?

He ignored her question. 'We had an agreement!' he rapped. 'No cosy twosomes with the opposite sex.'

'Cosy twosome!' she exploded. 'He was a client!'

'Huh!' Gideon grunted, clearly not believing her. She could have hit him.

'We were discussing business!'

'It looked like it!'

'We were having a business dinner!' Why the Dickens was she bothering to explain? It was his jugular that should be gone for, not hers!

'From where I was standing, another half-hour and you'd have been *eating* each other!'

'How dare you?' She might have said more, but a look of such fury came over his expression that her words dried in her throat as he came forward, and she backed away.

'That's where you've been, isn't it?' he demanded. 'To your flat. To...' Enraged, he grabbed her wrists. 'While I've...'

'Don't talk rot!' she yelled. 'And don't judge me by your own over-sexed standards!'

'Over-sexed!' Gideon let go of her wrists as though her skin burned him. Then he shook his head, as if not quite believing any of this.

Ellena took the opportunity to get in quickly before he could draw breath. 'I went to my flat, yes—but alone.' And, enraged with herself suddenly, she continued, 'Why the devil am I explaining any of this to you? You're the one in the wrong, not me!'—and saw straight away that Gideon hadn't taken very kindly to that.

'Me!' he roared. 'I'm not the one who's out half the night playing the field.'

'Playing the field!' Oh, she so nearly hit him then. 'Listen, you!' she snapped furiously. 'If Cliff Wilkinson is interested in anybody, it's my boss, not me. My boss, incidentally, who was scheduled to come with us, only she got flattened by a migraine attack at almost the last—' Ellena broke off—she was explaining! Dammit, she was explaining, when she should be going for his throat! 'Don't you ever do anything like that again!' she told him off well and truly.

Much did it bother him! He didn't bat an eyelid but was instantly and aggressively firing at her, 'You couldn't ring? You couldn't let me know in advance that—'

She was not going to have blame put at her door—she was not. 'I rang Mrs Morris!' she cut him off short.

Those slate-grey glistening hard eyes narrowed. 'You're not married to Mrs Morris!' he snarled icily.

'With luck, I won't be married to you for much longer!' she hurled back.

His look went from icy to arctic. 'We're stuck with each other and you know it!' he clipped curtly, and it was obvious to Ellena from his remark that he was more than a little fed up with their arrangement. 'You do anything to jeopardise my claim to my brother's child, and—' He

broke off when Ellena, her fury abruptly de-
parting, was left feeling defeated suddenly, left
feeling most unexpectedly dangerously close to
tears. Hurriedly she turned her back on him.

'I...' She tried to speak, but was too full of
emotion and found she needed all her strength
to battle to regain control. She'd just die if she
broke down in tears while Gideon was there.

She was still striving for control and wishing
the Gideon would go back to his own room and
leave her when, to prove that he was still right
behind her, his hands came to her shoulders.

She could feel his touch, warm, firm but
oddly gentle, through the cream silk of her
blouse. He turned her to face him. She didn't
want to look at him, but seemed compelled to.
From unhappy blue eyes she looked up, fully
expecting to see him tough and aggressive but,
to her surprise, she could see not an atom of
aggressiveness about him—and, even more sur-
prisingly, there was nothing in his steady gaze
but understanding.

'You've been so brave,' he said softly. She
shook her head, denying, wanting to tell him
that he was the rock she leaned on.

'No,' she whispered, their argument, its
cause, suddenly meaning nothing. Gideon still

had his hands on her shoulders as, instinctively, she put her hands on his waist.

She tried to smile. It was a poor effort. Gideon bent his head, and kissed her. It was a gentle yet lingering meeting of mouths. His arms came about her. She put her arms about him, and as their kiss broke she laid her head against him for a few moments.

Then she looked up into warm slate-grey eyes. Gently, tenderly, slowly, with their arms still about each other, they kissed again. And, as that dreamlike kiss ended, Ellena looked up at Gideon once more. All her anxieties seemed to vanish while she was in his arms and she felt she wanted to stay there for ever. But—this would never do.

She stepped back, her arms falling away from him. Gideon's hands were now at her waist. 'Goodnight,' she said huskily.

'Will you be all right?' he asked.

'Yes. Fine,' she answered.

He searched into her eyes for perhaps ten seconds longer. Then, 'Goodnight, my dear,' he said, and left her.

CHAPTER SIX

ELLENA awakened on Thursday morning and without conscious thought touched her fingers to her lips. Never had she known a kiss as gentle. Giving, comforting—little short of wonderful.

A sound in the next-door room brought her fully awake. It was Thursday, a work day, she hadn't time to lay here dreaming. Swiftly she left her bed and headed for the shower. Yet—dreaming aside—she could not remove the feel of those tender kisses from her mind.

They weren't supposed to kiss, she and Gideon, not like that! And certainly not at all when it was not for the benefit of anyone watching, but just for the solace of each other. Oh, help, what was happening?

Ellena knew that they should not have kissed, but yet—it had seemed so right. They were both in their own way, and privately, quite desperately trying not to believe that the worst had happened to their siblings. But it had only taken a mention of his brother's child—her sister's child—for her to fold.

Ellena left her shower and got dressed, knowing that their gently exchanged kisses had been a warm consoling of each other, no more. Just an attempt to soothe their inner disquiet.

But, having fairly logically disposed of any questions that had been aroused by the fact she had felt she had wanted to stay in his arms for ever, Ellena recalled how she had flown at him to start with. Had that been her, normally quiet, calm and even-tempered yelling at him? Heavens above, she was starting not to recognise herself!

Abruptly, wearing a blue suit and crisp white shirt, Ellena left her room. She was halfway down the stairs, though, when she suddenly started to feel all churned up inside at the thought of seeing Gideon again.

She swallowed hard on nerves she didn't know she had and made herself go on. She went briskly, matter-of-factly, into the breakfast room. Gideon was already there. He lowered the paper he was reading. Quickly she went to her usual seat.

There was no sign of the housekeeper. 'Good morning,' Ellena greeted him primly.

Gideon did not take up his paper again but put it from him and studied her for a moment, before, to her dismay, he said sincerely, 'I was out of order last night. I apologise that...'

'You're apologising for those kisses we—' She broke off. They were kisses she wanted to remember—she felt bitterly let down that he was saying sorry about the comfort given and received.

But—she'd got it wrong! And, it seemed, Gideon was annoyed that she could think the way she had. 'You expect me to apologise for something that was warm, and spontaneous—and beautiful?' he demanded sharply.

He'd thought that too! She didn't care that he was cross with her. 'You know, Langford, if you tried really hard, I could quite get to like you,' she answered mischievously.

Gideon stared at her, his glance going to her mouth tugging up at the corners. His own lips started to twitch—and Mrs Morris came in. He was still looking at Ellena when he stood up. 'Bye, sweetheart,' he murmured, planted a husbandly kiss on her cheek and, picking up his paper, he went.

Went, leaving Ellena wondering about this new person inside her who had stirred into life since knowing him. The person, the imp who, without her volition said things like '...if you tried really hard, I could quite get to like you'.

Ellena passed a few pleasantries with the housekeeper, but when a little later she left the breakfast room herself and started up the stairs, she suddenly started to wonder about something else. Every morning, on leaving her room, she would, without fail, go up to the nursery. This morning, with thoughts of Gideon Langford so much in her head, her visit to the nursery had gone completely from her mind!

Having rectified that omission, Ellena drove to work in a pensive mood. Cool it! sprang to mind. Gideon was taking up too much time in her head of late. Their marriage had nothing to do with feelings for each other, but was a necessity for their own ends, and she must remember that. Quite why she was giving herself this lecture, Ellena was unsure. She should not have to remind herself that the sole and only reason she and Gideon had gone through that marriage ceremony was in order to ensure that—should it come to it—some judge would consider they, with their joint family tie to Violette, would be a better choice to be her guardians than Russell and his avaricious wife.

Determining that never again would she put her arms around Gideon and enjoy the strength of his arms about her—and kissing when no one else was around was *definitely* out—Ellena

parked her car and went to the offices of A.
Keyte and Company.

Her first port of call, however, was not her
own office. 'How are you feeling?' she asked
Andrea when she dropped in to see her.

'As good as new,' Andrea answered, and indeed looked it.

'Is it convenient for you to hear my report
about my meeting with Cliff last night?' Ellena
asked.

'No need.'

'No need?' Why was Andrea looking what
Ellena could only think of as a little bashful?

'Well actually, Cliff showed up here last
night.'

Ellena was intrigued. She went and took a
seat near Andrea's desk. She wanted to hear
more. 'He came here after I had dinner with
him? You were still here?'

Andrea nodded. 'I was feeling heaps better by
that time and was down in the car park and
about to drive home when Cliff turned up.'
Ellena was absorbed. Andrea went on. 'Anyhow, despite my arguments, he said I still
looked a degree under, and insisted on tailing
me home.'

'What a nice man he is,' Ellena commented.

'That wasn't what I was thinking when, every time I looked in my rear view mirror, there he was. Although...' Andrea hesitated for a moment or two, and Ellena thought she wasn't going to say any more. But, all at once, she started to confide, 'Although, when we left the bright lights behind, it suddenly started to be comforting to have Cliff's headlights in my rear view mirror. And, by the time we got to my place, yes, I confess it, I had started to think myself what an extremely nice person he was. And then, as we both got out of our cars, it seemed the height of churlishness when he was miles away from his hotel to give him a curt goodnight and leave him standing there.'

'You invited him in?'

'And was staggered when he insisted I put my feet up while he made me some sandwiches and something to drink. I'm amazed that a man could be so kind!'

Gideon was kind, Ellena found herself thinking when she went along to her own office. Grief! Stop thinking about him! Get on with some work, do!

Ellena went home that night still determined to cool it. Fat chance! Gideon seemed to have something on his mind and, while courteous to her in every way, he seemed to be too preoc-

cupied with his own thoughts to want to chat.
Fine, that suited her perfectly!

'I've an appointment in an hour,' he deigned
to inform her at the end of their meal.

Business, I trust! 'I'll say goodnight, then,'
she returned as coolly as she got, and, getting
to her feet, she headed for the door.

She had some work she could be doing.
Feeling perverse, she went and spent some time
in the nursery. Beverly was on duty that night
and Violette was awake with no sign of going
to sleep. Ellena was able to play with her for
some while.

Ellena saw very little of Gideon in the next
few days. They shared meals together but neither of them was very chatty, and the meals in-
variably ended with Gideon going to his study
and Ellena going to the nursery.

The weekend passed in that fashion and on
Monday Ellena drove to her office and owned
to feeling extremely down. She tried to lose herself in her work, but couldn't. She gave up trying when, at three that afternoon, her phone
rang, and she heard the all-masculine tones of
the man who was taking up far too much space
in her thoughts.

'Ellena?'

She recognised his voice at once.

'Gideon?'

'I've just had a call from home.' Home. What a lovely sound that was.

But, 'What's wrong?' she questioned urgently, instantly all attention.

'Nothing at all,' he straight away calmed her fears. 'Other than, as you know, Beverly's having an extended weekend off, and Marjorie Dale has just phoned to say her daughter has come home from university, upset about something or other and in need of a little tender loving care.'

'Marjorie wants some time off?' Ellena guessed.

'I've told her to take as long as she needs—she says she's sure to be back tomorrow. Meanwhile she'd had a word with Mrs Morris, who's said she can cope quite well on her own, but...'

He didn't have to finish. 'I'll go home now,' Ellena told him.

'You're lovely,' he said softly, and she felt warmed as much by the fact that it seemed there was a thaw in the coolness between them, as by his comment.

Nonsense! 'Goodbye!' she said crisply, and put the phone down and went in search of Andrea.

Ellena spent a delightful time with Violette, who was at her charming best. She was still in the nursery when, around seven that evening, Gideon came home and came up to see how she was faring.

'You seem to be coping,' he observed.

'A piece of cake,' she answered casually. 'Er—I forgot to mention to Mrs Morris... Would you mind telling her that I won't be dining downstairs?'

'I'll bring your meal up to the nursery,' he offered, not exactly weeping, she noted, that he was to be deprived of her company at dinner. 'I could have my meal up here with you,' he offered after a moment.

A smile beamed inside her suddenly. She at once denied it. 'You don't think that's carrying togetherness a little too far?' she queried coolly.

'I merely thought I might spend some time with my niece,' he replied, his chilly tone beating her offhandedness hollow—and then he ambled out.

That puts you in your place! Oh, what she would have given to thumb her nose at his back. Thaw, my foot! Her inner smile had died, but she wouldn't let him get to her; she wouldn't.

She smiled prettily at him when he delivered her tray, and thanked him nicely. No way was he going to know that his smallest remark had the power to hurt her.

'Oh, by the way...' she said just as he was leaving. He halted and favoured her with an aloof look, and Ellena almost told him to forget it. But, knowing him, he'd only want to know, 'Forget what?' and that would make too big an issue of it. 'I could do with some male muscle around half-nine, tennish.'

His aloof look disappeared. 'I'm intrigued,' he drawled when she hesitated to tell him why.

Beverly had a lovely self-contained apartment on this floor, but it was private. As was the large bed-sitting room which was allocated to Marjorie Dale. And, while there was an exceptionally good baby alarm which was plugged into the room of whoever was on duty, and Ellena could easily have transferred it to her own, she had not the smallest intention of doing so. Just as she had not the smallest intention of leaving the small mite to sleep on this floor all on her own tonight. And, since it was going to take quite some of Gideon's valuable time from his work in his study to have her double bed moved up to this floor, the answer was obvious.

But, feeling he would think her over-protective, Ellena grew belligerent, and let him know she was not going to take any nonsense when she informed him, 'Violette will be out of her cot for her last feed around that time. I'd like her cot dismantled and carried downstairs.'

Gideon seemed only a little less intrigued. 'Presumably, madam,' he mocked, letting her know he wasn't very good at taking orders— she had never supposed he was—'you'll want it reassembling elsewhere?'

'You know where my bedroom is, I believe,' she answered crisply.

And could have thumped him when he muttered something that sounded suspiciously like, 'Now, there's an invitation!' But his expression was bland when he went on to question, 'You're intending the infant should sleep in your room tonight?'

Ellena sensed trouble. 'You can put her cot in your room if you prefer,' she replied sweetly. But, brooking no argument, she told him fiercely, 'There's no way the little one is going to sleep up here on her own!'

He stared at her flashing blue eyes. 'You're a dragon!' he accused.

'No, I'm not!' she denied.

He smiled suddenly—her heart flipped crazily. She wanted to smile back. 'Did you fight your sister's battles like this?' he wanted to know.

Tears sprang to her eyes. She looked away. Who else in the space of moments could have her laughing and crying? 'Clear off!' she ordered.

'And we haven't been married a month!' he sighed—but went. And Ellena no longer felt like crying, but wanted to laugh.

Beverly had told her that Violette slept all through the night now. By the time she had the baby settled and asleep in her room, Ellena was ready to sleep the night through herself. A tiny scrap Violette might be, but it was amazing how much energy was required to cope with all her needs.

So why, if she was so tired, couldn't she sleep? Ellena lay in her bed willing sleep to come. But it evaded her. She tried to make her mind a blank, but all she kept thinking of was Gideon. Tough, cool, sharp—smiling. Hateful, icy, aloof—charming. Who else did she know who could so easily change her mood? No one. His grin, his laugh—oh, drat the man!

She had heard him come up the stairs, making as little noise as he could, in view of the baby in the next-door bedroom. He'd have been asleep for ages by now! Were it not for her infant guest, Ellena felt she would have put her light on and read a chapter from a book or something. Her only option was to lie there.

It was around three o'clock when she finally drifted off into a deep, exhausted sleep. But only to be dragged rudely half awake at half past three by a light in the room—which *she* hadn't left on.

'Ellena!' She came a little further awake to hear her name spoken. 'Come on, wake up!' the male voice urged. 'It's been crying, and it's wet!'

Ellena came fully awake. She opened her eyes fully. Gideon was in her room, the centre light was on and he had Violette in his arms. Poor love, how long had she been crying and she hadn't heard her? Instinctively she wanted to go and take charge. She controlled the instinct. He wanted to spend more time with his niece. Let him!

'Change her, then,' she said prettily, and, closing her eyes, snuggled down.

'Aw, come on, Ellena!' he pleaded.

Beg! She opened her eyes again. He was robe-clad, as she'd seen him once before—and didn't look at all comfortable as he awkwardly held the damp bundle. 'Ask me nicely,' she suggested, all huge eyes and innocent.

'Please!' he said.

Ellena was considering his request when the matter was settled for her. The baby started to cry—and instinct could no longer be denied. In a flash she had whipped her bedclothes back.

She saw Gideon's glance leave her face and go to the thin, almost transparent material of her nightdress, her pink-tipped breasts seeming to momentarily fascinate him. A small squeak of a sound escaped her as she rapidly whipped the sheet over her again.

Gideon was the first to speak, his glance back on her face again, easing her embarrassment as he offered, 'Can I do anything to help?'

'You can shut your eyes for a start!' she snapped, and had chance to get herself together when he presented her with his back. 'Give her to me,' she said when, out of bed and decently robe-clad, she was ready to take charge.

It took all of a half-hour to get the baby attended to. To his credit, Gideon just didn't return to his own room and leave her to it, but did all the fetching and carrying Ellena needed from the nursery. And when Violette was once more comfortable and nodding off to sleep, he held the baby while Ellena tidied away and washed her hands.

'Bliss,' Ellena whispered, the infant back in her cot again and looking positively angelic.

They stepped away from her cot and, the communicating door open, Ellena switched on her bedside table lamp and went and snapped off the main bedroom light switch. There was still ample light coming from a lamp in Gideon's room. She felt sensitive to him for some reason, and quietly apologised, 'I'm sorry Violette woke you.' A hard worker herself, she was very much aware of how tired he must be. 'I didn't hear her crying.'

'I thought all women had an inbuilt baby alarm,' he replied softly.

'Mine must be on the blink,' she whispered lightly, and prepared to wish him goodnight—only somehow he came nearer to go to his room, and since she was still by the light switch and the communicating door, they somehow seemed to bump into each other.

He automatically put out a hand to save her from a stumble—his touch electric! 'Ellena!' he murmured—she wasn't sure that she didn't breathe his name, too. What she was sure about was that she didn't mind one tiny bit when, as if compelled, Gideon started to draw her to him.

Gently they kissed and instantly she felt her heart ease. His strong arms came around her thinly clad body, and he held her to him. Ellena's arms seemed to go round him of their own accord. Gideon broke his kiss and looked down into her bemused face.

His head came down again, his lips once more on her own. Yet, something different was there. His kiss was gentle still, but something—was happening—and Ellena welcomed it.

Gideon's arms about her grew firmer; he moved her with him through the doorway and into his room. And suddenly the tenor of his kisses was changing. While still giving, his lips were also demanding.

Ellena was happy to give. At least, she thought she was. There was no thought in her head telling her to back away, at any rate, so taken up was she in the thrill, the passion of his kisses. She had no notion that they were moving, subtly moving, towards his bed. Again and again they kissed, and then Gideon was gently moving her to lie down.

He did not leave her, but lay down with her, his body next to hers, his wonderful hand caressing her shoulders, his kisses to her throat making her want to arch herself closer to him.

Ellena followed her instincts and pressed herself against him. She heard a kind of a groan escape him, and started to feel nervous that, just as Gideon had ignited a fire within her, she seemed to have power to do something to him too.

His hand caressed to the firm fullness of her breasts. 'Gideon!' she breathed—and pulled away while she had a modicum of strength.

Immediately he removed his hand from her breast. 'Am I going too fast for you, sweetheart?' he asked softly.

It was the endearment that did it! He had called her sweetheart before, but only so Mrs Morris should hear and think them head over heels in love. 'I—I don't think this is a very good idea,' Ellena gasped, struggling to sit up.

There was one terribly tense moment when she thought Gideon might not let her go. But let her go he did—and then she half wished he hadn't. 'Up to now, your manners have been impeccable,' he grunted.

'It's not done to feel yes but say no?' she queried.

He gave a short bark of laughter. 'At least you're not denying what you feel,' he commented. After the way she had clung to him she didn't see how she could! Anyhow, she had an idea he had sufficient knowledge about women to know exactly how she was feeling. 'Just denying me,' he added—but, she noted, not sounding very unhappy about it.

He got off the bed and reached down and helped her off it. 'Are you going to forgive me my appallingly bad manners?' she asked.

'Never,' he replied.

Briefly, they kissed. His hands tightened on her waist. He gave her a small push. It was what she needed.

'Goodnight,' she said, and swiftly left him, hoping that, though he knew all about women, he had no idea of how she yearned to be with him always.

There were not many hours to go before she got up and started her day. She spent them in wonder at this all-consuming love for Gideon that had come to her unsought, and also in earnestly hoping that she could get through this marriage and divorce without him ever discovering the depth of her feeling for him.

How she had come to fall in love with him she had no idea. She supposed, thinking back, that something had started to stir in her that day he had called at her flat and had spoken of marriage. She had thought he meant marriage to someone else and, she easily recalled, she hadn't liked it.

Ellena felt torn in two: she loved Gideon, but he didn't love her, and would probably die laughing at the very idea. She tried to find rest in sleep. She had just nodded off when Violette decided that she wanted to start her day. Ellena went over to the cot, picked Violette up and hugged the lovely, precious bundle to her.

Ellena was late getting to her office—she would have been surprised if she'd been on time! She was busy with Violette so didn't get down to breakfast until after Gideon had left for his office. He had poked his head round the communicating door to tell her he was off— Ellena, feeling decidedly pink about the ears, had kept her head bent and doubly concentrated on the baby.

'I—may be late this evening,' he'd remarked.

'Fine,' she'd answered, loving him with all of her being.

He had gone and she'd taken the baby with her to the window and watched, catching a glimpse of his good-looking face as he'd steered his car to the front of the house and had gone down the drive.

She was still at the window with Violette when she saw Marjorie Dale hurrying up the drive. Beverly was due back this afternoon. Everything was getting back to normal—though since her discovery of her love for Gideon, Ellena felt things would never be normal for her again.

'Are you sure you should be here?' she asked Marjorie Dale before she handed Violette over. 'Your daughter…'

'She's fine,' Marjorie beamed. 'Hannah's a home-loving girl and felt in the need of a bit of reassurance. I've just seen her off now, but she'll be home again in no time when her university term ends. She wanted some of her mum's cooking and a cuddle to keep her going until then.'

What a lovely family they must be, Ellena mused. For all she had been late in, she sat staring out of her office window, her thoughts on anything but her work. Marjorie had said she'd get Ted Morris to give her a hand with taking the cot up to the nursery… Ellena wanted Justine home, home safe. Wanted her family back. Ellena took heart when she recalled how Gideon had once warmed her by saying that she was family. How generous of him to say that—the thought of marrying had not occurred to him then. How kind he… Gideon was back in her head.

She'd had a late start, she was tired, and Gideon kept coming between her and her work. Ellena was still trying to catch up when Andrea popped in and a business discussion followed, during which Andrea revealed that one of the small and discreet out-of-the-way hotels they did some work for had been in touch and were anxious to have some of their books back.

'I was working on that account only half an hour ago,' Ellena smiled, and, since the hotel was on the way to her flat, she offered, 'I'll drop them in if you like.'

'They're a bit short-staffed, or they'd send someone over.'

'No problem,' Ellena assured her.

Nor was it. That was, delivering the books and having a small and friendly conversation with the pleasant woman who did the hotel's books amongst a dozen other jobs, was no problem. What was a problem, though, a most infuriating one, was that, having left the book-keeper's office, briefcase in hand, Ellena walked back through the hotel and, in the open lounge area on her left, saw the man she was married to sitting in deep and absorbed conversation with a most stunning brunette!

Barely able to believe her eyes, Ellena stopped dead in her tracks. This wasn't the kind of hotel Gideon would normally use; she would swear to it! So what was he doing in this out-of-the-way, small but discreet type of establishment? Ellena reckoned she knew full well what he was doing there, and such a feeling of fury and sickness engulfed her at that moment that she was barely conscious of what she was doing.

'I may be late this evening,' he'd said. Now she knew why! What she should do, Ellena knew full well, was to get out of there before Gideon turned round and saw her. No chance! Besides, Gideon was so taken up with what the brunette was saying, Ellena reckoned that the ceiling could fall in about his ears and he'd never notice it.

And that made her angrier than ever. But it was the sick feeling in the pit of her stomach that was her prime motivator as, sick beyond bearing, Ellena took a left turn into the lounge area.

Gideon looked startled to see her. Well, he would, wouldn't he? He thought she was miles away, playing happy families! He rose to his feet; tall, good-looking, and he was a swine—a swine, swine, swine, and she loved, loved, loved him.

'Hello, darling,' Ellena smiled, ignoring his companion—to hell with manners! 'I'm in something of a rush,' she beamed at his surprised countenance. 'I couldn't get you at the office, but, if you see Nanny before I'm home, would you remind her that our baby alarm isn't working?' That would settle his hash! Explain that, Daddy!

She was out of there before he had chance to draw breath. Not that he was likely to introduce the brunette!

Ellena was in her flat before she had cooled down sufficiently to start to be appalled by what she had just done! Oh, no, she hadn't, had she? The fact that there was still no communication from her sister had taken some of her steam away but, as the minutes after that slowly ticked away, Ellena owned that what she'd done had been totally crass.

Only then, when anger had departed, leaving only that sick feeling in its wake, did she realise what it was that had motivated her back there at that hotel, what that sick feeling was. She had been jealous! Unthinking, unseeing, acting on pure, blind, outraged jealousy. Oh, Lord—now what?

Well, she couldn't return to Oakvale, that was for sure. She thought of Violette. Well, not for a while anyhow. But she wouldn't be surprised if it had gone midnight when Gideon came home. And, cringe though she might, there didn't seem any good reason why—when, because of the baby, she was going to return anyway—she shouldn't go home now.

This love she bore Gideon had turned her world upside down. Never had she known she was capable of acting as she had. She'd have said she hadn't a jealous bone in her body—but look at her!

Ellena set out for Oakvale, unsure quite when the house had become home, and the flat she had always considered home had become 'the flat', but she had more serious things on her mind during that drive. What in creation was she going to say to Gideon the next time she saw him?

As she had anticipated, and she was sat on thorns until she knew for sure, Gideon had not arrived home yet. Ellena went through all the motions of appearing as if everything was normal. She went up to the nursery and spent some time with Violette and Beverly, asking everyday questions about the baby's welfare, about Beverly's welfare. She left the nursery to go to the dining room, even managing to eat some of her meal and appear as if none of it was about to choke her.

But, when she retired to her room that night, she was still no further forward with regard to what sort of an excuse she could give to Gideon—and she did not mistake that he would come looking for one, because of her jealous outburst.

It was about eleven o'clock when she showered and got into her night things and calculated that since she wouldn't see Gideon until the morning she'd better use these in-between hours to think up something. Whatever happened, he must never know that jealousy had been the root cause.

It was too late now to wish that she hadn't done it. She had an idea that Gideon admired her honesty, and she valued his good opinion. But what honesty was there in telling him, in front of a stranger, that their mechanical baby alarm was broken when it wasn't? When it was only his reference last night to the female, built-in baby alarm system—hers had manifestly failed to go off—that had brought forth her outright lie.

At eleven-fifteen, and in utter desperation to forget that she had been jealous for an instant, Ellena went back over conversations, events and happenings—and, at last, felt she had something which might wash to explain her behaviour.

He'd done something similar to her, if she remembered rightly. That night she'd had dinner with Cliff Wilkinson to discuss business, Gideon had been furious because he thought she'd broken their agreement and was out on a date. Well—couldn't she claim the same thing?

In Gideon's case, of course, it *was* a girl-friend, *and* a date. Obviously he was still concerned that his sister-in-law might have her spies about—hence the small, out-of-the-way hotel. Dastardly rat!

Gideon had once suggested that she'd be hell on earth once she got going—well, she couldn't argue that. Never would she have believed she could have acted the way she had tonight—oh, what had he thought? What was he thinking?

She was still sitting up in bed hugging her knees—what point was there in lying down when sleep was light years away?—when suddenly, into the silence of the night, she heard his car coming up the drive. Hastily she put out her bedside lamp. The light from his headlights swept her room. Oh, grief!

She heard him quietly enter the house. Perhaps he'd go and make himself a cup of coffee in the kitchen or something? But no. She heard him coming up the stairs—and realised she was barely breathing, which was ridiculous, she owned, because she wasn't going to see him that night. That communicating door would stay closed until just before she left for work in the morning, when *she* opened it.

With her ears tuned to the direction of that communicating door—just in case—Ellena had the shock of her life when, not having bothered to go into his own room first, Gideon came along the landing and entered hers.

'Oh!' she exclaimed in utter shock, her heart threatening to leap out of her body when, without so much as a by-your-leave, Gideon came in and switched on her bedroom light.

'Forgive the intrusion,' he apologised—oh, heavens, had there been a faint emphasis on that word 'intrusion'? 'I spotted your light on a minute or so ago—I didn't think you'd be asleep yet.' And, having taken away any excuse she had to protest, he stared at her for some long seconds, and then quietly said, 'Would you mind telling me what all that was about back at that hotel tonight?'

Oh, help! What had she planned to say? She couldn't remember! Ellena all at once became conscious of her flimsy attire and pulled the covers closer around her—she was still sitting and stayed that way, knowing she would feel far more vulnerable than she was already if she lay down.

'It's your prerogative, is it?' she somehow found the wit to challenge. He'd done something similar—that was it! 'Your *tête à tête* wasn't over dinner, though no doubt dinner followed.' Stop it, stop it, you're starting to sound jealous! 'Forgive my fib about the baby alarm,' she ploughed on—*attack, attack*—'I just wanted to establish that we both play by the same rules.'

'You think I was out—partying?'

'Whatever you like to call it,' she offered sarcastically.

'You're wrong!'

And the moon was made of Gorgonzola! 'Go on, tell me—you were putting Violette's name down for Cheltenham Ladies' College!'

Gideon moved away from the door, came nearer to her bed and stood looking down at her. Ellena didn't think she liked that very much. 'No,' he answered, his eyes scanning her face.

He made her nervous—help her, somebody! *Attack.* 'No?' she tossed back at him, anything rather than he should discover how dear he was to her, how very much she loved him, how green-eyed and sick she'd been to see him with the stunning brunette. Ellena got her second wind. 'Well, stap me, Sir Percy,' she taunted, 'if she wasn't your girlfriend—and it was *you* who stipulated we have no friends of the opposite sex, I believe, then...' She hesitated. He was still standing over her and she *was* feeling vulnerable. 'Then—oh, I know,' she went on, refusing to be browbeaten, 'it must have been our divorce lawyer.'

Oh, heck, what had she said? Up until that point she had been unable to read anything in Gideon's expression, save that he seemed determined to get to the bottom of her behaviour. But, at her last remark, his face darkened—and she could not mistake that he was exceedingly angry.

'You can forget *that*!' he snarled, so angry that he snaked out an arm, his right hand taking a hold of one of her wrists as if to underline his decree. 'I haven't...'

'Let go of me!' Ellena exploded in sudden panic. 'I don't care what you have or haven't. If...'

'Then you damn well should. This is about...'

'I know quite well what it's about!' She refused to let him dictate the terms. She might love the man with an intensity that had shaken her, but no way was she going to stay quiet and let him steamroller her. 'It's about you not needing as much "rest"—if you'll pardon the euphemism—as you thought. Well let me tell you something, Langford, if...'

'You don't know what you're talking about!'

'I may not have your superior brain, but I play fair!'

'What the hell do you mean by that?'

'Just that if I—um—abstain as part of our agreement, then it's unfair that…'

'How can you abstain from something which you've never tried?' he wanted to know, his fury all at once seeming to ebb, mockery taking its place.

There was no answer to that. 'You're still holding my wrist,' she complained.

His answer was to reach down and take hold of her other one. And, thus manacled, she glared at him. Much good did it do her! 'You were saying?' he mocked—and she wanted to hit him.

Wanted to hit him—and hold him. Oh, Gideon—she felt helpless. 'You're hurting me!' she stretched the truth a mile—and gained nothing, for Gideon did not let go his hold on her, which was what she had been after. But, coming to sit on the side of her bed, he gently brought her wrists to his mouth, and, one after the other, he kissed them. Her heartbeat was already in overdrive. He had to let her go; he had to! Just a simple kiss to her wrists; just the fact of his lips against her skin seemed to be scrambling her brain power. 'Okay, so you've kissed and made it better—now go to bed,' she ordered, with what strength she had left.

Gideon stared at her for some moments, then with the very devil suddenly appearing in his eyes, he replied, 'Not until you kiss me, and make *me* better for the hurt you inflicted.'

She loved the way his mouth curved up at the corners, as if caught by some amusement. 'I never touched you!' she denied.

'You hurt my feelings.'

'How?'

'You accused me, unfairly, of breaking our no dating agreement.'

'She, the beautiful brunette, she wasn't—er—a rest cure?'

'You're a cheeky baggage,' Gideon informed her. But added what she wanted to know. 'It was—business of sorts—trust me.'

Ellena's heart instantly lightened. She wanted to believe him. In that moment of having him with her, of his seeming so sincere, she wanted to give him the benefit of the doubt.

'You win,' she smiled. 'Take it that I've kissed you better.'

'Oh, Ellena Langford—what do you take me for?' he reproached her, and while she was wallowing in bliss because he'd called her Ellena Langford—albeit that Langford was now her name—Gideon, still holding her wrists, pulled her gently to him and placed his mouth over hers.

And Ellena, her heart racing, knew that she should pull back. Knew it as soon as Gideon broke that kiss—but, somehow, she just could not. Nor, it seemed, could Gideon.

Their lips met again, unhurried, gentle still. And again they gently broke apart. 'G-goodnight,' she said—but seemed too trans-fixed to move backwards.

'Goodnight,' he replied, moved but a fraction away—and then, with a strangled kind of groan, took her in his arms.

Ellena went willingly, his touch, the feel of him as she put her arms about him, sending all logical thought fleeing. Gideon kissed her, drawing the very soul from her. She kissed him back and was enrapt, enchanted.

'Little love,' he called her, and she was float-ing.

She wanted to cry his name, but his mouth was over hers again. She wanted to get closer to him and stretched towards him, mindless of where the bedclothes were. She felt the warmth of him, felt burned by it, was enflamed by him.

Gently his hands caressed her back, his touch through her thin covering sending her into further raptures of delight. He held her yielding body to him—oh, utter bliss!

His hands caressed her shoulders as he kissed her and drew her very soul from her. She was vaguely aware that at some time his jacket and tie had been disposed of, and as he tenderly lay her down and came to lie down beside her, their feet entwined and Ellena realised that he had parted with his shoes and socks also.

'Sweet Ellena,' he breathed, his fingers in her hair, his body so close to hers. 'Sweet, sweet, Ellena.'

Her bones went to liquid. She melted under his touch as the caress of his fingers moved over her face, her throat. 'Gideon,' she whispered shyly, and loved him when he looked understandingly into her eyes, those wonderful direct slate-grey eyes seeming to say, Trust me.

And trust him she did. Tenderly he kissed her throat, her shoulders; he was aware, it seemed, of her every shy reaction. 'Don't be alarmed,' he soothed when his caress ing fingers moved the thin strap of her nightdress down her arm.

'I'm not,' she smiled, and basked in his smile of encouragement which came a moment before he bent his head and traced gentle kisses from her shoulder to her breast.

Though she did clutch onto him when he captured her naked breast in his mouth. But the fire he had ignited started to burn out of control when, with his mouth, he moulded the swell of her creamy breast and its hardened pink tip, and she wanted more.

'Gideon,' she called his name.

He kissed her breast, and, raising his head, he smiled, 'Are you all right?' he asked softly, when she felt sure he must know that she was.

'Oh, yes,' she breathed and—for her, extremely bold—she confessed, 'I want to kiss you too.'

His look was gentle, understanding completely as he discarded his shirt. It was an utter joy to her to feel his naked chest beneath her hands. Side by side they lay together. She bent her head and kissed his nipples.

She looked up and was about to tell him that she loved him—only he kissed her. A kiss that demanded, received, and then gave so much. Ellena was lost in the wonder of it all.

Then their kiss broke. And, with shock, she realised that she hadn't a stitch on. 'What happened to my nightdress?' she questioned on a strangled gasp of sound—and Gideon grinned.

'Sweet love, you wriggled just a little—and I helped.'

She loved his grin but, shy again suddenly—and how she could be defeated her—she stayed close to him. Then discovered that somehow he had managed to remove his trousers. 'Did I...?' she questioned, as her bare legs mingled with his.

'I managed that by myself,' he murmured, and all was silent for a while then, as they kissed deeply.

Ellena felt his hands caressing her skin, and sighed with love and longing when with gentle fingers he caressed her breasts. She wanted to call his name again—but felt too full of love and longing to speak.

He raised his head, his eyes resting on her nakedness. 'You're so, so beautiful,' he breathed.

'Oh, Gideon,' she whispered—and, shyness getting the better of her, she rolled onto her side and against him, hiding her curves from his view. For some long moments they stayed like that, Gideon understanding of her reticence and not pushing her at a faster pace than she was happy with.

Together, breast against naked breast, legs entwined, feet caressing, they looked at each other. He kissed her, a tender, giving, small kiss. He held her in his arms, one hand straying to gently stroke the rich contour of her left buttock.

'Are you going to be mine?' he smiled down at her.

Her heart was near bursting with happiness. 'I—I want to be,' she answered nervously. 'But...'

'But?' he questioned, that hand on her behind stilling, warm and wonderful. She wanted to tell him that she didn't know how things went from here, that she was frightened that he might be disappointed that she didn't know very much. Well, she knew nothing, if it came to that. 'You're not going to go all bad-mannered on me again, are you?' he softly teased.

And Ellena so wished that he hadn't. Because it brought back memories of last night. And it was just as if, like last night, he had called her sweetheart again. 'Sweetheart'—that meant nothing to him. As this, their lovemaking, meant nothing to him—whereas it meant the whole world to her.

She kissed him, knowing that was getting in the way of feeling. She wanted to give and give, to be his—but 'sweetheart', his insincere 'sweetheart' was pounding in her head.

'What's wrong?' Of course, as she might have known, Gideon straight away sensed that something was very much amiss.

She took her arms from him. 'You're going to hate me,' she said chokily—and hated *him* when, lightning-sharp on the uptake, it seemed it was beneath him to attempt to persuade her against her wishes.

Though his voice was far from even, when, rolling away from her, he grunted, 'May I suggest that the next time you feel like committing yourself—sweetheart—you have your timing checked!'

And, with that word 'sweetheart' hanging so powerfully in the air as Gideon left her bed, Ellena felt it was beneath *her* to change her mind and, as her body still demanded, attempt to persuade him to stay.

CHAPTER SEVEN

NEVER had a night seemed so long! Out of sheer exhaustion Ellena realised she must have slept at some time, but she was awake long before dawn, and was again fretful.

Gideon had swallowed the explanation she had given him for her behaviour in that hotel last night. And, by now knowing something of the man he was, she had accepted, and trusted him, when he'd assured her that he and the brunette were discussing some business.

Jealousy tried again to get a grip—Ellena ousted it. She must believe him. Trust him—which was not why she was wide awake and fretful. She had kissed him and, from the love she bore him, had wanted to make love with him. And he, Gideon, had kissed her and had wanted to make love, only—he did not love her. He felt something physical for her, yes, but it was not love.

And she wanted him to love her—but she might just as well cry for the moon. Because he did not, and was never going to, love her. And so much for guarding her secret—she was terrified that in her responses to him last night she had given away something of how very much she loved him.

Ellena came out of the mental torment of her thoughts when she heard the muffled sound of movement coming from the next-door room. By the sound of it, Gideon couldn't sleep either.

To get up and start her day didn't seem a bad idea. At least it would give her something to do, something else to think about.

As if... Gideon was in her head the whole time she was in the shower, and all she had achieved when she was dressed was to realise that she would have time to spare—time to spend with Gideon over breakfast!

Grief, no! She had no idea how she was going to face him, much less spend a leisurely breakfast with him! She could, she suddenly realised, leave without breakfast. Cowardly perhaps, but might she not feel better able to face him when she'd had a day away from home, conversing with other people, putting in a day's work...?

Ellena knew she wasn't fooling anyone but herself. The way she was feeling now, she was never going to feel any better. She waited three minutes after she heard Gideon leave his room, then went and opened the communicating door. Then, briefcase in hand, she went up to the nursery. Gideon sometimes had to leave home earlier than usual—she didn't see why she shouldn't, too.

Beverly and Violette were busy starting their day, and Ellena guessed she would be interfering with routine if she stayed too long. Even so, she only left the nursery when she judged that Gideon would be deeply absorbed with his newspaper. For the look of the thing, she would have to pop her head round the breakfast room door.

It should have been easy. So why did she feel all trembly inside and little short of a nervous wreck as she approached the breakfast room door? She swallowed hard and, wanting to go in any direction but the one in which she was going—she entered.

'Good morning!' she said brightly to his raised newspaper and, recalling how last night she had lain naked in his arms, felt herself go scarlet—oh, why did she remember that now! Gideon lowered his paper, his gaze taking in her flushed face. A gentle smile began to take shape on his mouth. Ellena rushed on. 'I want an early start,' she explained, waving her briefcase in his general direction. 'Pending file, overflowing!' she explained—and would have got out of there—only Gideon was on his feet and was starting to come over to the doorway where she stood.

'Ellena, about last night…' he began—and she nearly died. Did he *have* to?

'Tell you what, Gideon,' she managed, still somehow holding her bright tone, 'you promise never to do that again, and I'll…' she was backing out of the door as she spoke '…and I'll promise not to go where—er—I've never been before.' With that she turned and, as if her pending file was the most important thing on her mind, rushed out to her car.

Gideon was in her head all the way to her office. '…about last night…' he'd started to say. What had he been going to add? 'I'd like you to forget it'? 'Never do that again'? 'Whose bed shall we try next time'? Grief, there wasn't going to be a next time. She'd take jolly good care of that. And, anyhow, after the two times—once in his bed, once in hers—when matters had started to get out of hand and she had politely declined, was it likely Gideon would want to bother a third time?

Ellena's pending file was as she'd left it, empty save for information she was waiting on and could not take action without. Even so, she intended to have a far better day today than she'd had yesterday.

An intention that abruptly got away from her. Indeed, it went straight out of her head when, just after ten that morning, her office door opened. When her visitor did not at first speak, she dragged her eyes away from her computer—and nearly fainted with shock.

'Gideon!' she gasped, the computer instantly forgotten, her mind in a spin. Apart from anything else—how had he got past reception? Why hadn't Lucy warned her? Irrelevant! 'What are you...?' Ellena's voice faded. He looked stern, serious. Her mind started to race—so much for her dashing away from the house that morning. There was no escape. Gideon had seen her love for him—he'd come to bluntly tell her...

'May I?' He took hold of a chair and, bringing it close to where she was sitting, he sat down next to her. And while she was desperately striving to summon up some sort of a defence, Gideon went on to make her extremely agitated, when he started, 'Last night...'

'Last night,' she echoed as firmly as she was able, and while she was searching for something else to add Gideon continued, and she discovered that a defence was not needed.

'Last night at that hotel,' he went on—and she wished that she had not interrupted him.

Jealousy, that cursed, wretched emotion which she wanted no trade with, but which since its introduction would not, it seemed, leave her alone, was picking at her again. 'You weren't there on business?' she queried coolly, memory of the lovely brunette burning bright in her mind's eye. But—Ellena was puzzled—why would Gideon come to her office looking so serious just to tell her he'd lied last night?

'It was business—of sorts, as I said,' he answered.

'She—the lady you were with—' Ellena's tone was off hand—he'd never know the effort it cost '—she was more—er—friend than business connection?'

Gideon shook his head and, those serious slate-grey eyes holding hers, he said quietly, 'Ellena, my dear, Mrs Turner is a private detective.'

Ellena's eyes shot wide, his quiet, 'my dear' startling enough without the rest of it. 'A private detective!' she exclaimed, her mind darting off in all directions. Pamela Langford was having them watched, as he'd intimated she might? 'A private detective looking like that?' she exclaimed out loud, her question regarding Pamela getting lost under her feeling of shock.

'I thought they were all long raincoats and headscarves too,' Gideon agreed. 'I suppose, in some cases, Mrs Turner being the opposite of what one would expect might achieve better results. But that's beside the point,' he went on, the sternness of his expression relenting for a moment. 'I've had a highly recommended detective agency working for me from the beginning.'

Ellena strove hard to keep up. '*You* employed a detective agency—not Pamela?'

She guessed her confusion must be showing, for it was quickly and quietly that Gideon explained, 'I wasn't ready to believe that my brother was dead.' Ellena was instantly all attention now—nothing else mattered.

'You said you'd employed this agency from the beginning?' she questioned tautly, knowing that he would employ only the best.

'From the first.'

'And?' There was more—there had to be if this was the reason Gideon had come to her place of work to seek her out!

'At first nothing. Then a detective stationed in Austria found someone who'd seen a couple answering to Kit and Justine's descriptions having drinks in a bar with another couple, the night before the avalanche struck.' Ellena's mouth went dry. 'Time passed and no more news came through, but I insisted the detective stayed there, stayed to ask questions. Then someone was found who belatedly remembered seeing four people looking like the same quartet in a car heading south the next morning, the morning of the avalanche.'

It wasn't much to go on. Indeed, it could be absolutely nothing to go on; Ellena saw that. But she latched on and refused to let go of the fact that Gideon wouldn't be here with her now telling her this much if it wasn't relevant to something. 'Is that all?' she questioned huskily, refusing to believe that it was. Not now!

'For an age it was—though I've received scrappy bits of information which amounted to nothing. Then last evening I was between meetings when I took a call on my car phone from Mrs Turner, who'd just landed after a case conference in Spain.' Spain! 'She indicated she might have something of interest to report.'

Ellena felt her colour draining away. 'You met at…'

'I was on my way to a meeting in connection with a takeover we're planning. But that could wait. This was far more urgent. I said I'd like to see her straight away, and she suggested the mutually convenient hotel where you saw us.'

Oh, grief, what a pain he must have thought her—rattling on about the baby alarm! But, as Gideon had himself intimated, this was more important than any of that. 'What did Mrs Turner have to say?' she asked hurriedly.

'She started by saying that the trail had gone cold, but that they'd an excellent man in Austria who daily called at the hotel my brother and your sister were staying in, and that he'd made friends with the staff.'

'And?' Ellena asked again.

'And, in so doing, learned of an inconsequential happening concerning a ''Mrs Pender'', who telephoned from Spain having apparently left the hotel without settling her account. The view was that some other poor hotelier had been left nursing an unpaid account because ''Señora Pender'' had never stayed at his hotel. But the detective thought it worth a mention when he phoned through with his daily report.'

Ellena could hardly speak. 'You think it was Justine?' she questioned hoarsely. 'You think it was her phoning from Spain?'

'Mrs Pender—Miss Spencer? A long shot but, to a foreign ear, during a bad telephone connection from Spain to Austria? Not forgetting you were certain your sister would never leave a hotel without paying her account.'

'She wouldn't! I know her.' Ellena's mind raced on. 'It could be that she thought Kit had paid, and he thought that Justine had.'

'And that when she discovered differently, she phoned the hotel straight away,' Gideon finished for her.

'You believe it, don't you?' Ellena questioned tensely.

Gideon stared into her strained tense and ashen face. 'I'm—starting to,' he said slowly. 'I had another telephone call from Mrs Turner a short while ago.'

Her mouth went dry again. 'You've an address—a phone number?'

'Neither,' he said at once. And, before revealing what his phone call had been about, he warned, 'Now don't hope for too much. Mrs Turner rang a minute before I left my office to come here to tell me she'd just received information that a man by the name of Langford is on a flight from Barcelona.'

Ellena stared at him. 'Kit's on—a plane—now!'

'It may not be him, so neither of us must hope for too much, but…'

'Neither of us?' she questioned chokily.

Gideon looked at her steadily. 'He's not travelling alone,' he said succinctly.

She so desperately wanted to believe it was Kit and Justine, but Gideon had said that neither of them must hope for too much. How could she not? 'This man—his travelling c-companion—is female?' she questioned.

'She is,' Gideon confirmed.

'What time are they due?' she asked, unsurprised to find that they had both left their chairs and were now standing.

'I'm on my way to the airport now,' he answered, adding quietly, 'I came to collect you.'

'Oh, Gideon!' she whispered shakenly, and it somehow seemed totally natural that they should for a moment go into each other's arms—that they should support each other in this moment of extreme stress.

She felt him place a light kiss in her hair, then he was taking her by the arms. 'Come on, love,' he said gruffly.

By the time they reached the airport Ellena was in a dreadful state of anxiety. She barely remembered leaving the office. She had a vague memory of seeing Andrea, of Gideon introducing himself and alluding to her ashen face, explaining that his wife wasn't well and that he was taking her home. It passed her by that this hardly explained to Andrea what he was doing at the office to begin with.

Ellena was barely aware of the drive to the airport either. Though she did recall almost asking him why he hadn't thought to tell her any of what he knew before. Then she also recalled that the only chance he'd had to tell her anything about his meeting with Mrs Turner had been when he'd come to her room late last night. Perhaps it had been his intention to discuss it with her then—only they'd kissed and—oh, grief! She wasn't likely to remind him of that!

The wait for the Barcelona flight seemed endless. 'It may not be Kit and Justine,' Gideon warned when they saw from the arrivals board that the plane had landed.

'I know,' she agreed, as another interminable wait ensued and she mentally followed the passengers through passport control, baggage reclaim and customs.

The first of them started to come into the arrivals hall, and she found she was hanging onto Gideon's left hand as if it were a lifeline. Yet she couldn't let go.

Then she saw them! Justine and Kit were yards away, arms around each other, as happy and unconcerned as ever they were. Ellena realised that some kind of sound must have escaped her. Because, although Gideon had spotted the errant pair too, he pulled her against him for a moment.

'All right?' he queried.

'Never better now,' she said, and thought that this must be one of her happiest moments when the man she loved looked down at her and, taking out his snowy white handkerchief, gently wiped away a stray tear she didn't know had escaped.

It then became urgent for both of them to get to their relatives and touch and feel, and just be heartily overjoyed, when they could have been forgiven if they'd accepted that they would never see the pair again.

'Ellena-Ellen! Fancy seeing you here!' Justine exclaimed, in high spirits, but obviously glad to be home as the two hugged each other. 'Have you got your car? We left ours at h—' She broke off, suddenly realising that Kit had been greeting a man unknown to her.

'Gideon, you don't know my fiancée,' Kit was saying, and while Ellena was getting used to the fact that it seemed her nutcase of a sister was now engaged to the father of her child, Justine was shaking hands with Gideon and asking how come he and her sister were at the airport to meet them.

There was a lot Gideon could have said and, now that the agony of not knowing if they were alive or dead was over, he could have been for-given for finding release by reprimanding the pair of them for what they had put Ellena and himself through. But, since both Kit and Justine appeared blithely unaware of the fear endured in their absence, Ellena felt that she had never loved Gideon more when, with a glance to her, he answered mildly, 'It's a long story. We were a little worried about Violette, so you could say we joined forces to look after her.'

'She's all right?' Justine questioned a touch frantically. 'My baby's all…?'

'She's fine,' Gideon assured her. 'She's being very well looked after at Oakvale…'

'She's at your home?' Kit chipped in. 'What happened at Pamela's? Every time we phoned she said the baby was blooming. She…'

'You phoned Russell's wife?' Gideon ques-tioned grimly.

'Like every week,' Kit answered—and, with a grin to his fiancée, continued, 'It would have been every day just lately, if Justine could have got to a phone—came over all mumsie, didn't you, love?'

Justine hit him, and they all laughed together. The four of them made a general move towards the airport car park—and Ellena, overjoyed to the point of tears to see her dear sister again, at the same time coped with fresh shock when Justine revealed she had been about to telephone her too, one time, after she'd rung Pamela. 'Only Pamela told me you'd only just left after one of your regular visits to see Violette—so I knew you wouldn't be back at the flat yet, even if I did ring to say hi.'

The four of them were in Gidcon's car on their way to Oakvale. Justine and Kit were extremely excited at the prospect of seeing their daughter again and taking her to their home while Ellena struggled with the fact that Pamela Langford had known Justine and Kit were alive!

All this time, while she and Gideon—each in their own way—were going quietly demented, Pamela had known that Justine and Kit were safe and well! All this while she and Gideon had been through their own private hell needlessly!

Hard-nosed! It was little short of criminal! Not only had she lied about Ellena's regular visits to see Violette, Pamela had even made out that she was still looking after the baby!

Gideon had felt that she had given Violette up too easily—now they realised why! Pamela had known for a while that Justine and Kit would be coming back, doing away with the ne-

cessity of a guardian for their child, and there-
fore there was nothing to be financially gained
by trying to get Violette back. Criminal—she
had been downright wicked!

'We've decided to get married!' Kit's an-
nouncement cut through Ellena's thoughts.

Though, before she could find the words to
offer her congratulations, she heard Gideon offer drily, 'While it goes without saying, Kit, that
you're a very lucky man—what brought this
on?'

Both Justine and Kit laughed, though it was
Kit who, suddenly serious, replied, 'Justine gave
me one hell of a shock, that's what!'

'I—er—went a bit broody,' Justine explained.
'We were in Austria when we bumped into
some friends of Kit's who were driving to
France the next day. So we went too, and had
a whale of a time. Then Nick's father wanted
his boat sailing down from Marseilles to
Gibraltar, and Nick said he could do with some
extra crew. Anyhow, it seemed a good idea at
the time—to volunteer, I mean—only, then I
started to get a terrible longing to see Violette,
to be with her. But I didn't like to tell Kit and
spoil his fun.'

'And I thought, when Justine went in for long
silences, that she'd gone off me. It took me

about a week to pluck up courage to ask what I'd done wrong.'

'And he looked so hurt—I just had to tell him it wasn't his fault, but mine, and that I was just homesick for Violette, and wanted to be a proper mother.'

'And that was when I knew I wanted to be a proper father—a married one, but only to Violette's mother.'

There did not seem to be much more to say after that. 'Congratulations,' Ellena smiled, and the rest of the journey seemed to be taken up with talk of the baby, of the wedding which would take place as soon as Justine and Kit found a house to buy.

Though Justine did remember to thank Ellena and Gideon for looking after their offspring. 'I expect the neighbours complained when you took Violette to your flat to live,' she opined to Ellena. 'How clever of you to contact Gideon. I had an idea you disapproved of my farming her out on Pamela in the first place.'

'Some aunts are like that,' Ellena answered. Violette was obviously the centre of Justine's universe just then, and, while it pleased her that her sister's maternal instinct had finally arrived, Ellena saw no point in telling Justine about the avalanche, of which she clearly knew nothing.

Nor about the other matter, which of course Justine knew nothing about either—that she and Gideon had gone through a marriage ceremony in order to safeguard Violette's security, caring and happiness.

Gideon must be seeing things the same way, Ellena realised, for he was saying nothing on the subject either. In fact, given that Justine and Kit were babbling away, there was little room left for other conversation, so he was saying scarcely anything at all.

'May I go and find Violette?' Justine asked when they pulled up at Oakvale—and was first out of the car.

'Of course.' Gideon smiled. And to his brother, 'You know where the nursery is.'

Ellena stared after them as, hand in hand, Justine and Kit took off. She got out of the car and went to follow them, but was startled when Gideon, placing a hand on her arm, stopped her.

She halted, looking at him, and loved him so much. 'Happy?' he asked.

She nodded. 'Relieved, oh, so very relieved,' she said. 'You?' she asked.

'Torn between a desire to give Kit a manly hug and box his ears for what the inconsiderate pair have put us through.'

She knew the feeling. 'When was it ever any different?' she smiled and, as he let go her arm, they walked side by side into the house—where peace had ceased to reign.

'Isn't she gorgeous?' Justine cried from the first landing, Violette in her arms, Beverly hovering nearby. 'Can we go home now?' Justine, it appeared, wanted her baby and Kit to herself, and was not the least interested in lunch or any sort of refreshment. Gideon took charge.

In no time at all, he had intervicwed Beverly, who was about to lose her charge. Then, between them, he, Kit, Ellena and Beverly were carrying a whole mountain of baby equipment out to Gideon's car.

'There's no room for Ellena!' Justine objected when, the car boot full, other bits and pieces took up the available space inside.

'I shan't need any,' Ellena smiled, and, as it suddenly dawned on her, 'There's no reason why I should come too!'

'Will I be all right?' Justine asked, as if suddenly nervous that she might have forgotten how to care for Violette.

'It's like riding a bike,' Ellena promised.

And, reassured, Justine beamed, 'See you, then—and thanks. Thanks, Beverly.' Then she gave all her attention to the little darling she had so yearned to see.

'Bye, Ellena—we'll be in touch,' Kit said, getting into the front passenger seat.

Ellena stepped back, and Gideon, his large car full to capacity, paused before he got into the driver's seat. 'I'll see you when I get back,' he said, those direct slate-grey eyes steady on her blue ones.

And all at once Ellena felt shy, tongue-tied. 'Drive carefully—Uncle,' she said—and wanted to die from sheer mortification because he might think her remark was as ridiculous as she felt it to be.

She stood with Beverly and waved them goodbye. On turning and heading back into the house, the superb nanny declared, 'I'd better go and tidy up the nursery and pack.'

'I'm sorry,' Ellena apologised.

'Oh, don't be,' Beverly smiled. 'I've loved working here, being here, but I won't have a problem being redundant—I'll soon get something else. And your husband has been most generous with my severance pay.'

They went up the stairs together in pleasant conversation and parted when Beverly carried on up to the next landing. Ellena went along to

her own room and went to stare out of her bedroom window.

She loved the view of lawns and shrubs and
trees. She, like Beverly, loved being here. She...
Oh! Suddenly, painfully, screaming out of a
dark unwanted somewhere, Ellena only then
realised that Beverly wasn't the only one who
was redundant! That—with Violette gone—
there was no earthly reason for her and Gideon
to remain married. With a sick feeling hitting
her, Ellena all at once realised that her marriage
was over!

Swiftly on the heels of that thought came another dreadful realisation—that she too must be
expected to pack and be on her way! Oh, good
heavens, what on earth was she doing day-
dreaming out of the window, thinking of how
much she loved it here at Oakvale, Gideon's
home! He had said 'I'll see you when I get
back' but wasn't that his way of saying, I won't
expect to see you when I get back?

Ellena realised that her love for Gideon might
have made her over-sensitive where he was concerned. But, while she had seen an extremely
kind side of him which gave a small percentage
of doubt that he had meant anything at all by
his parting remark, there was absolutely no denying that Justine and Kit's arrival home most

definitely spelt the end of her marriage to
Gideon.

Her pride gave her a kick-start when Ellena
saw that the odds were Gideon would not expect
to see her there when he returned. Come to that,
this being a working day, he might not return at
all but could well go straight from Kit's to his
office. Ellena, her car still at her office, rang for
a taxi.

With a heavy heart she left her room and went
to say goodbye to Beverly and to wish her well
in the future. Then, having been unsure whether
to pack and go, or whether to return for her belongings when Gideon had explained matters to
his staff—and, of course, come back when she
knew he would not be around—she started to
feel edgy. She was growing more and more con-
vinced that Gideon would wait only to unload
his car at Kit's flat, and he would then go
straight to his office. But, just in case he did
plan to return straight away to Oakvale, Ellena
decided to leave now.

She still felt emotional about Justine and Kit's
safe return. Loving Gideon the way she did, she
just didn't feel up to discussing their divorce
arrangements just yet.

She went to the drawing room to wait for her
taxi. She would ring Gideon, perhaps come for

her things at the weekend. By then she would be emotionally stronger—more able to cope. Yes, it would be far better to contact him over the phone, when she wouldn't see his dear face, far better to discuss their divorce never having the chance to see him again, when he would not be able to see the sadness in her eyes that might, in an unguarded moment, be there. Never was he to know how deeply she loved him.

Gideon, and the fact that she would never probably see him again, was very much on her mind on the taxi ride to her flat. Her heart was somewhere down in her boots when she suddenly remembered that Justine and Kit intended to marry. She would see Gideon at their wedding, she realised. Though, by then, since their siblings didn't appear to be in any particular hurry to wed, Ellena was hopeful that she would have perfected a friendly—if perhaps just a trifle offhand—technique when next she saw Gideon.

She supposed that at some time Justine and Kit would get to hear that she and Gideon had married and why. That was another area she must guard, to make sure that Justine, so close to her in some ways, picked up not the slightest hint that she had come away from this marriage so achingly heart-sore.

For a brief while Ellena thought of Justine and Kit, and how the two of them now seemed a little more grown up. Ready to take on the responsibilities of marriage and a family life. Ellena realised that she must take a back seat in Justine's life. She would always be there for her; that went without saying. But Justine had Kit now, and both of them were ready to commit to each other.

By the time the taxi dropped her off at her flat—somehow returning to her office just did not figure in her list of priorities—Gideon was back in her head—where he was to stay. For no matter how much she decided to think positively, to think of her future, of the endless possibilities, sights to see, things to do and hear, she always seemed to come back to thinking about Gideon.

Think positively, she asserted to herself yet again. Then the phone, which had been silent for so long, started to ring. Gideon! Oh, stop it! It would be Justine... Ellena picked up the phone.

'Hello,' she said lightly.

'You didn't go back to your office, then?'

Gideon! Her heart started to hammer, adrenalin rushed. 'Did you?' she managed.

'I said I'd see you when I got back,' he reminded her evenly.

'Oh, sorry, I must have misunderstood.'

He could have taken her up on that—she was glad that he didn't. Though she owned to being completely thrown when, after a moment or two of saying nothing, he abruptly asked, 'When are you coming home?'

'Er...' Words failed her. Home! Hope started to soar high. 'I'm—not.' She quietened ridiculous hope.

The pause that followed was electric. Then Gideon commented, 'Your belongings are here.'

And Ellena fell to earth with a bump—all too obviously, now that they had no reason to stay married, he didn't want her belongings cluttering up his home.

'I was going to ring you and suggest I come over at the weekend to collect them—I'd have brought everything with me today,' she went on to explain, 'only I wasn't sure how you wanted Mr and Mrs Morris told, or Marjorie and...'

'The weekend will be fine,' Gideon cut through her lengthy explanation, and while Ellena's spirits sank lower and lower she knew all too plainly that she had read the situation correctly: he wanted her bedroom cleared. Because, quietly, he put down his phone.

Well! Goodbye to you, too! Who did he think he was? she fumed indignantly. Not even the courtesy of, 'It's been nice knowing you', did she get! Well, could he go sky-diving without a parachute!

She wiped at her damp eyes—she wouldn't cry over him; she wouldn't. Instead she busied herself tidying an already tidy flat, and dusted everywhere. Then she went and took a shower and washed and dried her hair.

Having donned a pair of jeans, she had just finished buttoning up a crisp white overshirt when her doorbell sounded. Gideon! Don't be ridiculous! Her start of alarm was flattened by deadly dull common sense. She went to answer the door, beginning to feel guilty that she hadn't rung Andrea to tell her about the safe return of Justine and Kit. If memory served, Andrea had an appointment with a company out this way later today. She wouldn't put it past Andrea to stop by to see if she was feeling any better.

Ellena had the door unlatched, and was about to open it, when suddenly and alarmingly it hit her that Andrea fully believed her to be no longer living at her flat, but at Oakvale with Gideon!

It wouldn't be him—why on earth would it be? But, too late now, the door was ajar. She pulled it open—and felt colour rush to her face. She dug her nails into her palms, desperate for control.

'Hello,' she said brightly. 'I didn't expect to see you before the weekend!' And not even then if she couldn't control her emotions better than this—she was inwardly trembling!

Gideon stared at her, his expression unsmiling. 'You and I, Mrs Langford,' he said after some moments of tough scrutiny, 'have some unfinished business.'

That 'Mrs Langford' told her all she needed to know. Gideon, never a man to let the grass grow—ever a man to get things done—had come to talk about their divorce!

She came away from the door. 'You'd better come in,' she invited.

CHAPTER EIGHT

'WOULD you like something to eat? Have you had lunch?' Ellena asked, leading the way into the sitting room. Keep calm, civilised. For heaven's sake, theirs wasn't a proper marriage, never had been, was never meant to be; so there was no need for recriminations or apportioning blame at its ending.

'I've more important things on my mind than food,' Gideon declined her offer shortly.

He looked serious, she saw. In fact, quite grim. 'Er—take a seat,' she invited, holding back the urge to offer him coffee. She needed those few moments alone, by herself, moments in which to get herself together—but there was no guarantee that he wouldn't follow her to the kitchen. Gideon walked over to an easy chair, but waited until she was seated on her sofa first before he sat down. 'Did Justine and Kit get settled in all right?' Ellena asked politely after some desperate moments of trying to find something natural to say. Oh, heavens! There was a determined sort of glint in Gideon's eyes.

242

'I don't know,' he answered, those eyes holding hers, 'I didn't stay around that long.'

'You went straight back to Oakvale?' By all means, let's keep this polite.

He nodded. 'Where you weren't!' he commented succinctly.

Why should she feel a need to swallow? Because he was so dear to her, that was why. She loved him so much. But it was time to sever all ties with him, time to stop pussyfooting around. 'It's a great day—Justine and Kit coming home,' she remarked. 'Though there was no need for you to come here in person—our lawyers can sort out the details of our annulment, and...'

'You don't think we should discuss it a little first?' Gideon cut in grimly.

Ellena stared at him in some surprise. What was there to discuss? 'You want alimony?'

His lips twitched briefly, no more. 'I once called you a cheeky baggage,' he recalled.

'You bring out the best in me!' she said off the top of her head, and found she couldn't keep her eyes off his wonderful mouth, the mouth that had wrung from her such an ardent response of which she had never dreamed herself capable.

'Sex aside...' Gideon remarked, and while she dragged her gaze from his mouth she was

having forty fits inside that he had so easily
hopped on to her wavelength. '…we married,
you and I, from a cold necessity. But, Ellena,
my dear—' his voice softened '—I like to think
we found a—friendship—if you like, a
warmth…' he seemed to be selecting his words
very carefully '…that rules out a cold and impersonal divorce.'

Her blue eyes were fastened on his now. They
would divorce, naturally they would. Gideon
was not saying that the divorce was ruled
out—just that, from where he saw it, it would
not be cold and impersonal.

She smiled; she just had to. Gideon had as
good as stated that he felt a warmth and a
friendship for her. 'You've been a good friend,'
she acknowledged, 'there for me when I needed
a shoulder.'

'It was mutual,' he answered.

'I helped you—during the long, painful waiting?'

'It was a comfort to hold you in my arms,'
Gideon confessed. But proceeded to shake her
rigid when, quite deliberately she felt, he added,
'That was, initially. Later I found there were
many times when I just wanted to take you in
my arms, and hold you.'

Ellena blinked, her eyes growing wide. 'For our—er—mutual strength—comfort?' she sought clarification.

Gideon studied her attentive expression. 'Partly,' he agreed. 'But more, I think, because I could barely help myself.'

She coughed lightly; her heart was hammering away. Don't be ridiculous! She shouldn't read anything at all into what Gideon was saying. 'Sex aside,' she tried to quip, 'you...'

'You're a desirable woman, you know that,' he stated. 'But I don't think sex had a great deal to do with those moments when I had to make myself turn from you. Those moments when I had to resolve to keep away from you, to shut myself in my study.'

Ellena took a shaky breath. She knew he liked honesty, but she wasn't sure that she was up to taking much more of this without giving something of her feelings away.

Pride was a wonderful ally. 'So that was why I gained the impression you'd gone off me—that first weekend we were married,' she attempted to tease lightly.

'I'm encouraged that you noticed my absence,' Gideon answered, far too astutely for Ellena, causing her to realise that she was going to have to watch every word while this divorce conversation lasted. She opted then not to answer at all, for fear that she might reveal even a fraction of her feelings for him, sealing her lips—that was, unless she absolutely had to answer him. 'You're not going all cool and uppity on me, are you?' My heavens, was there ever a man who was not letting go!

'When did I ever do that?' Ellena felt that was a safe enough reply.

'Hopefully only when you, like me, felt it might be an idea to back off.'

'You're talking in riddles.' She denied to herself that she had ever, for a single moment, thought, Cool it, Ellena, or that he was taking up too much time in her head.

'So I'll go back to the beginning,' he decreed, when she would far rather that he wouldn't. 'You were really suffering on that plane ride out to Austria.'

'We both were,' her tongue disobeyed the embargo she had placed on it not to speak another word.

'And when we reached our destination the news was not good,' he went on. 'Which, fear being the animal it is, had both of us trying to hold down on the aggression that it triggered.'

'I let go of mine in that hotel room where Justine and Kit had been staying,' she recalled.

'And apologised at once,' Gideon took up, having instant recall, it seemed.

'You suggested I might call you by your first name,' she was right there with him.

'When actually what I felt, when you looked at me with those beautiful but unhappy blue eyes, was an absurd urge to cradle you in my arms.'

'Did you?' she exclaimed, astonished.

'Nothing sexual,' he assured her.

He didn't have to. 'I know,' she said, and felt she was going all to pieces again when he smiled gently at her.

'You've a lovely mind,' he murmured.

Ellena didn't know about that. What she did know was that Gideon talking this way, about her beautiful eyes and lovely mind—without that softening in his expression—was making it not a scrap easier for her to hide how much his every word and look affected her.

'You—er—were going to go back to the beginning,' she reminded him, desperate to keep the discussion impersonal—but realising too late that she hadn't wanted him to go back to the beginning either. She owned up to herself that just having him here muddled her thinking.

'I still am,' he assured her, and resumed, 'So we returned to England, and I soon discovered that you couldn't care less that Kit, or his heiress, would shortly be quite wealthy, and that the only reason you wanted guardianship of his and your sister's infant was for love of the child.'

Oh, grief, was Gideon saying that he—liked her? Ellena felt that he was—or was that all part of her being muddle-headed? 'You wanted Violette too,' she reminded him, feeling a need to take the conversation away from herself. 'You were prepared to marry to get her,' she added, though she wasn't terribly sure why she had added that, except she was feeling decidedly jumpy and was still anxious to have their talk moved away from herself; this astute man she had married might see too much.

'All very true,' he agreed evenly. 'I'd already worked out, before I consulted my lawyers, that I'd be better placed to win guardianship of Kit's offspring if I was married rather than single.'

'Should I feel honoured that you chose me?' Oh, Ellena, watch that tongue, do! She forced a smile. 'You must know quite a few other females who'd be willing—' She broke off when she saw Gideon start to smile.

'You were almost on your way to flattering me,' he observed with a charm which sank her.

'Well, you're not *all* bad,' was the best she could manage. 'So—um—you'd realised you'd better marry?' she prompted. Far better, she realised, to encourage him to talk than to converse herself when her tongue was proving so unwary.

'Reluctant though I was, it was an obvious solution,' he owned. 'The problem, as I saw it then, was—since I wanted to be certain I could as easily get myself unmarried—who did I know who would go along with it?'

'You realised Ellena Spencer would be easy to get rid of?' Ellena inserted—and inwardly cringed at the tart note that had crept into her voice. Oh, buck up, do! Any minute now, if she didn't watch her step, Gideon was going to realise that she was taking all this much too personally—already he was looking at her sharply.

Ellena gave an inner sigh of relief, though, when it seemed he had not noticed the acid in her tone, for quite pleasantly he acknowledged, 'You were the infant's aunt, and because of your love of your sister and the babe, you were as determined as me to have her. The decision was as good as made for me. And it should,' he went on, after a moment or two of just looking steadily at her, 'have been as simple, and as easy, as that.'

She stared at him, her blue eyes fixed on his slate-grey ones. She still felt jumpy, nervy. But there was a question begging to be asked here. 'Only—it wasn't?' she asked.

'It wasn't,' Gideon agreed. 'Logically, it was the obvious solution. But...' He paused, and then, again deliberately, added slowly, 'I discovered there's little room for logic when the emotions became involved.'

Her heart leapt—what was he saying? Idiot—idiot! He was saying that in a very short space of time he had gone from not knowing so much that his niece existed, to caring for Violette. His emotions weren't involved with *you*, Ellena berated herself, and strove hard to keep her voice even when, since it seemed Gideon was waiting to hear what she thought of his last remark, she forced a smile and conceded 'It would be a hard heart who couldn't be won over by one of Violette's smiles.'

'The young lady has a way with her,' he concurred—though he caused Ellena no small agitation to her heart when he corrected, 'Though it was more her aunt I was referring to.'

'Oh,' she said. There was no answer to that but—oh, foolish love—she wanted to hear more. 'Er—you mean—um—last night, when we—er—um—kissed?' Ellena's heartbeat quietened down as she realised that there was nothing to get very excited about. It was, after all, despite his remark about 'Sex aside', nothing but the physical desire that had sparked between them to which he was referring, with his comment about 'emotions involved'. Wonderful though those minutes in his arms had been.

'I mean last night,' he confirmed, flattening any of her wayward hopes—but only to arouse them again a second later when he quietly added, 'I mean, everything.'

Everything! Sorely did she wish she knew what he meant by 'everything'. 'You're obviously referring to our—um—Violette's very early alarm call yesterday when—er—things started to get out of hand the first time,' she managed to finish the sentence she had embarked upon.

'I don't know about getting out of hand,' Gideon grunted. 'It seems to me more that, of late, things between you and me have been growing more and more impossible.'

She had to admit he was right. From starting with an occasional kiss on the cheek when someone else was around, twice yesterday they had kissed when no one else was around, and had been extremely unrestrained. 'Well, you have been ''resting'' for rather a long while now,' she reminded him, wondering where the heck—when she was as tense as could be—that imp of mischief had come from.

'Sometimes, madam,' Gideon observed, 'I see the very devil in your eyes.' As long as that was all he saw! 'But this,' he went on, his expression suddenly extremely serious, 'is about you and me—and...'

'And our divorce,' Ellena finished for him— and at once saw him go from extremely serious to extremely angry.

'To hell with a divorce!' he snarled. 'You're married to me, Ellena Langford, and that's the way you'll stay!'

She stared at him in amazement. What had brought this on? But, while she might love what he said, she disliked very much the tone in which he said it. 'And to hell with you!' she erupted, both of them now angrily on their feet at the same time. 'We married for a specific reason; that reason has now gone! *We split!*' she informed him, glaring at him, loving him, desperately wanting him to cradle her in his arms, as he'd revealed he had wanted to that first night in Austria. But she was not prepared to be spoken to like that by any man—a girl had her pride! 'First thing tomorrow, I shall see my lawyers about getting this marriage annulled.'

'Impossible!' he rapped.

'Why impossible?' she flared.

'Because, by first thing tomorrow, this marriage will be consummated, and...'

Ellena was on her way to the door. 'Against my will! That's also grounds for divorce!' she exploded, not very certain of her facts, but panicking and ready to bluff it out.

She was about to open her door to show him out when Gideon, an angry Gideon, caught hold of her and spun her round. He seemed about to let forth a stream of something which she knew in advance that she would not like. Then, suddenly, all his fury vanished.

In an instant, perhaps seeing a flicker of fear in her eyes, all anger went from him. 'Oh, love,' he groaned, 'I wouldn't use force.'

What could she do? He sounded so anguished, and called her 'love'—Ellena just melted. As if they both needed a salve from the violence of their five-second spat, Gideon's arms came around her, and Ellena went into his embrace and put her arms around him.

'You probably wouldn't have to,' she whispered, remembering how last night she had wanted to be his.

She felt his kiss in her hair. 'One of the things I've always loved about you is your honesty,' he said softly.

Ellena felt near to tears. She swallowed hard. Then raised her head from his chest. 'Our—discussion seems to have lost its way,' she said.

'My fault,' he accepted. 'I've so much I wanted to say to you. And—perhaps because this is all so new to me—it doesn't seem to be coming out the right way.' He looked down into her warm blue eyes. 'I'd like to try again,' he requested.

Ellena stared up into his warm grey eyes. She didn't know what he wanted to try again. All she knew then was that pride no longer mattered. She wanted to hear him out. If during the time when they talked of a divorce—which for some reason he didn't seem to want at the moment—some of her love for him showed, then it no longer mattered. Ellena felt she knew enough of the man to know that, albeit that it might be unwanted, Gideon would treat her love kindly.

'Shall we go and sit down again?' she invited him to try again. She was still in his arms but, until he took them from her, she seemed powerless to move.

'May I kiss you?' he asked, something which, but for that harsh word 'force' still floating in the air, she guessed he would not have sought permission for. He truly was more sensitive than he let anyone see.

Her answer was to stretch up. Gideon's head came down and gently he kissed her—a kiss of such sweetness, almost love, she thought, that she felt quite choked that a man could be so tender.

She moved in his arms, her heart full. His arms fell away. 'Are you sure you wouldn't like something to eat, a coffee?' she enquired, desperately striving for some sort of normality. How could she ever have imagined that there was almost love in his kiss? She had better get her head together—and fast.

'Nothing, thanks,' he refused, but as she went to resume her seat on the sofa, 'You won't object if I sit here?' he asked. She shook her head, nerves biting when he came and shared the sofa with her.

'Do I take it that you—object—to our marriage being ended at the moment?' she asked, doing her utmost to stay calm—detached, if possible.

'Most decidedly, I do,' he confirmed.

'There has to be a reason?' she hinted.

'I could give you a dozen, but there's only one that matters.'

Her brain took off. 'Something to do with business?'

'No!' he denied emphatically. But, with a wry look to her, 'Lord knows how your mind works! We're talking about *us*, not business.'

Us? how wonderful that one word was. With difficulty—how easily he could scramble her thinking—Ellena got her head back together. 'You—make it sound—personal,' she said haltingly.

Gideon scrutinised her face for long moments. 'You don't think the fact that we're talking of our marriage, the fact of you being my wife, makes it personal?'

Ellena felt a lump in her throat, and was drowning in the beauty of hearing him call her 'my wife'. Oh, how dear he was, her husband. 'Well, if you put it like that,' she did her poor best to reply. And, gaining a little emotional strength, 'So why, Mr Langford, do you personally not want us to get unmarried at the moment?'

'You haven't guessed?'

She wanted to say something sharp like, I've lost my crystal ball, but she could not. There was just something in Gideon's expression, a warmth, a tenseness—could it be—a nervousness?—that flattened anything but her sensitivity to him.

Wordlessly, she shook her head. Then, huskily, she found her voice. 'I'd like to know,' she dared—and observed he looked more tense than ever.

But she it was who was tense and nervous when, after long, long moments of just looking at her, Gideon, as if under a great deal of strain, quietly revealed, 'My dear Mrs Langford, I have to tell you—when falling in love is not something I do—that I seem to have fallen in love with you.'

Ellena stared. Blinked, and stared at him. It was the last thing she'd expected to hear. That most wonderful sentence totally astonishing. 'Seem?' was the best she could manage, her voice cracking, not sounding like her voice at all. 'When?'

He ignored both questions, but sounded extremely unsure as he asked, 'You don't—mind?'

Mind! Were she able to believe him, she would be ecstatic. Though, when had he ever told her a lie? Oh, my... She swallowed, had the wildest urge to throw herself into his arms. But she loved him with all she had—which made it just too incredible that he should feel the same way about her!

'I—er—wouldn't mind hearing more about it,' she gave him the most encouragement she could manage.

'Is caution part of your accountant's training?'

'This isn't about business,' she tossed back at him. But, seeing that he still seemed under a great deal of strain, she relented a little. 'How much more encouragement do you want?' she asked, and again asked, 'When?'

'When did I start to fall in love with you?' Her misbehaving heart did a cartwheel; a few more comments like that and she didn't see how she would be able to stop herself from throwing her arms around him! 'As near as I can tell, and you've been in my head so much just lately, interrupting my work, my sleep...'

'You too!' she gasped.

'It's the same for you?' he questioned as quick as a flash, grasping a hold of her arms, seeming about to bring her closer. She wasn't ready!

'Forget I said that!' she backtracked fast.

'Not a chance!' he replied. But, when seconds passed and it seemed she was determined not to say another word, he reluctantly took his hands from her arms. Then he caught a hold of her hands instead, as if resolved that she was not going to move away from him until he had told her what she wanted to know, and had heard from her what he dearly wanted to know. 'On thinking it over and over, I've realised that I must have started to feel something different for you way back in Austria when, with Kit so much on my mind, I experienced that urge to cradle and comfort you. Then a few days later, when I rang you after you'd agreed to marry me, and I thought you'd been crying, I experienced a most definite pang. I didn't like at all the idea of you crying alone.'

'I discovered some time ago how sensitive you are,' Ellena said softly.

'Rot,' he denied. 'Well, perhaps where you're concerned,' he allowed. She smiled, and it seemed as though he would kiss her. Wanting to meet him halfway, Ellena pulled back instead. If he kissed her, she'd be lost, she knew she would, and, because it was so incredible that he might love her, she just *had* to hear more first. Gideon pulled back too, though he threatened, 'When I do kiss you, you're going to beg for mercy.'

'Never!' the imp who had recently come to live inside her body replied.

Gideon grinned, and her heart flipped. Oh, how she loved him. 'So,' he continued after some moments, serious again, 'there was I, denying that it mattered to any degree that you cried alone. Then the next time I rang you it was to hear you were getting cold feet about marrying me, and I told you I didn't think I'd forgive you if you stood me up—only to later realise, though barely knowing why then, that I somehow needed to have you in my life.'

Oh, how wonderful that sounded. 'Er—you didn't perhaps think your needing me in your life had something to do with you wanting to guard Kit's baby?'

'I was trying hard to be truthful with myself.'

'And me—will you be truthful to me?' she asked, purely because she had to.

'Especially truthful to you,' he answered sincerely. She smiled her thanks and, maybe because he was a man in a hurry to hear how matters were with her, and where he stood, he went on, 'So there we were, married, platonically—only there was I, constantly holding back on the urge to take you in my arms.'

'You—er—gave in sometimes,' she remembered.

'And didn't at so many others. You told me once that my charm was back—and I had such a near-irresistible urge to kiss you. But knew at once that I must not. We hadn't been married twenty-four hours and I felt you might feel you were in a vulnerable position.'

'That was thoughtful!'

Gideon's smile came out again. 'I confess I was feeling a touch vulnerable myself then.'

'You—were—um—starting to feel something for me, you said.'

'It was there, and getting more deeply entrenched. Which is why, of course, after we'd called here—that day we went nursery shopping—I so nearly kissed you again...'

'I wanted you to,' Ellena clearly remembered.

'Stay honest with me, my darling,' he breathed—and her bones melted again.

'I'll try,' she replied softly, and was truly starting to believe that—fantastic though it was—Gideon did, as he'd said, care for her. 'Go on,' she invited.

He gave her hands a gentle, but heartening squeeze. 'So there was I, wanting to hold you, only realising then that it was not just because we comforted each other when our spirits were low, but also because I somehow liked the feel of you in my arms. Anyhow, it was around then that I gave myself a talking-to on the fact that if I didn't watch my step I could end up in real trouble.'

'How?'

'I could, my dear, have found myself married for real.'

So much for wanting him to be truthful with her! 'That can easily be remedied,' pride insisted she should inform him.

'And you call *me* sensitive!'

Ellena had the grace to feel ashamed. 'Pardon me for interrupting!' she apologised—with a trace less acid.

Gideon said something that sounded like 'enchantress', but resumed: 'I then decided I'd better cool things—only, after a bleak weekend of keeping out of your way I drove you here to pick up your car on the Monday, and just had to give in to the urge to kiss you as we parted.'

'It wasn't because you thought there might be photographers around!'

He shook his head. 'You were getting to me in a big way. Later that day I went and collected Violette and could hardly wait for you to get home—which, even then, I thought was odd, because I wanted the infant for me, not you. It was only later that—having coped with my first experience of jealousy when you came home carrying a huge floral bouquet—as you held the baby in your arms, I experienced such a wonderful feeling of joy at seeing such happiness in your face as you thanked me. I answered, ''For you, my dear, anything.'' Then I realised it was true, that I would do anything for you.'

'Oh, Gideon…' she whispered.

And he smiled a loving smile as he told her, 'It was only a short step from there and I was starting to forget that it was only because of the baby we were together. I enjoyed having you living in my home; my heart lifted when you walked into a room; I enjoyed seeing you there, eating with you, hearing you laugh.' Ellena sat staring at him in wonder that it had been like that for him. 'Also wanting to comfort you when fear that you may have lost your beloved sister got too much for you.'

'Oh, Gideon,' she sighed tremulously.

'Do tell me you love me,' he urged. Ellena opened her mouth to speak, but was so choked, no sound came. Tenderly Gideon laid a butterfly kiss on her cheek. 'Do I have to tell you more about the effect you have on me? Of how heartily glad I was to hear your car on the drive the day I brought Violette home. The…'

'You'd phoned me here…'

'And asked if you intended coming home—and you snapped "How could I stay away?"—which left me deciding to be nicer to you.'

'Really? ''What's with the flowers?''' she reminded him of his greeting when she had arrived.

'I've told you—I was jealous!' She smiled;
she loved him so. He had been jealous?
Unbelievable, wonderfully unbelievable! 'So,'
he said, 'what have you got to tell me?' I love
you, she wanted to tell him, only he let go her
hands and caught a hold of her arms again.
'Your eyes tell me you do, but my darling, I so
need to hear you say it.'

'You—um—suspect that I do?'

He shook his head. 'Never in my life have I
felt so all at sea about anything. Sometimes I've
thought I've seen a little fondness for me in your
smile—others, I felt you didn't give a damn
about me. Yet were it not for that detective, Mrs
Turner, giving me the unsolicited information,
''Now there's a lady in love'', when you barged
into our conversation in that hotel last night, I
doubt I'd have this much confidence to reveal
my feelings for you.'

'Mrs Turner said that I...!' Ellena gasped.

Gideon nodded. 'Which made me wonder
how good a detective she was. To my mind she
was completely wrong. Only, this morning,
when she phoned with the news that Kit was
possibly on a plane on his way home—the

agency she works for living up to its excellent reputation—I began to consider that they were definitely in the business of employing somebody who was extremely astute in all aspects.' He paused, and took a long-drawn breath. 'So tell me, Ellena, was she right?' he demanded.

Ellena, looking at him, seeing that for all he must know how she felt about him—or she would never have let him get this far—seeing the look of strain still there in his dear face, suddenly folded. 'Who said to be jealous was your sole privilege?' she asked him softly.

'Darling!' He leaned forward and gently kissed her. 'Say it!' he urged. 'Put me out of my misery one way or the other. Say it.'

'Do you think I'm the sort of girl who'd go into a man's bedroom if I didn't love him?' she asked softly.

'God! I said you'd be hell on earth… *Say it!*'

She laughed; it was a joyous sound. 'I—love you,' she said.

She felt his grip on her arms tighten. 'And again, so I can believe it!'

'I love you, I love you, I love you!' she said—and knew he believed her, for the next she knew she was wrapped in his arms and he was raining adoring kisses down on her face.

For long, long minutes they held each other, and kissed each other, and just looked at each other, both too full for words. Then Gideon was kissing her again and telling her once more of his love.

'I'm having the same trouble you had in believing it,' Ellena whispered.

'But you do?' He kissed her.

She smiled. 'Oh, but I do,' she answered huskily—and was kissed again. And held tightly to his heart for ageless, wondrous seconds.

Then Gideon was pulling back to gaze adoringly into her loving upturned face. 'Never do I ever want to live again through an experience like the panicky uncertainty of these last few hours,' he said throatily.

Ellena moved to gently kiss him. 'Has it been so awful?' she asked softly.

'Nightmarish is understating it!'

'Not knowing if you would see Kit again—if it was truly him on that plane?'

'Not knowing, but having to face, if it was Kit, that I stood to *lose you*!'

Her breath sucked in on a gasp. 'Because there'd no longer be any need for you and I to join forces to protect Violette.'

'Exactly.'

'You thought of it *then*!' Ellena exclaimed.

'As you must have done.'

She shook her head. 'Not until after you'd gone to take Justine and Kit home did it dawn on me that my role as guardian—er—um—wife—was over. I was feeling a bit emotional, and not up to—er—discussing our divorce,' she owned.

'You really do love me,' Gideon said softly, as if still taking it in.

'Has it truly been so nightmarish?'

'Horrendous! One way and another I've been in hell ever since I've known how very deeply I'm in love with you.'

'I'm sorry,' she apologised lovingly.

'Which is why you're going to explain why you've given me such a hard time,' Gideon announced, but paused to give her a long, lingering kiss before he drew back to growl, 'Explain yourself, woman.'

Ellena laughed in pure delight. 'You're wonderful,' she told him, and absolutely loved being able to be this open with him. 'Er—where do you want me to start?'

'When did you know of your feelings for me?' he suggested without having to think about it.

'Um—I suppose, if I'm truthful…'

'I'll accept noting less,' he interrupted, taking a moment out to place a whisper of a kiss on her nose.

'Well, thinking back, I don't think I liked it too well when the day after we came back from Austria you came to see me and started talking about if you were married—and I thought you might be going to get married.'

'That was before I got around to suggesting that you and I should join matrimonial forces. You started to care for me then?'

He was wonderful; he seemed really eager to know. Ellena's heart swelled with her love for him. Though she had to shake her head and tell him, 'It wasn't anything as definite, as clear as that—just a feeling.'

'Go on,' he urged, much in the same way as she had done.

'Oh, I don't know,' she smiled. 'We married, and seemed to be getting on so well, that I started to get wary and decided to keep out of your way.'

'Self-preservation.'

'Are you always going to be able to read my mind?'

'I hope so,' he grinned, making her heart somersault. 'More, please,' he requested.

'Then—the night Violette arrived—so much for my notion of self-preservation—I remember feeling light-hearted and had to wonder if it was because you seemed light-hearted too.'

'You took your mood from my mood?'

'Must have.'

'That was the same night you niggled me by impudently asking if we now got divorced.'

'You didn't seem to go much on the idea,' she recalled, that impudence he had spoken of there again in her eyes.

'Why would I? You were starting to get under my skin. That was the night I suggested putting a desk in my study for you—you declined, saying you wouldn't dream of disturbing me—having no idea how much you were disturbing me already. And that was before I accepted that there was no way I was going to let you go if I could help it.'

'Oh, Gideon,' she sighed, his words utter bliss.

'I've got to kiss you—then you must tell more,' he breathed—and kissed her not once, but twice.

'You expect me to concentrate after that?' She emerged pink about her cheeks.

He grinned. 'Try,' he suggested mercilessly. 'I want to hear all your thoughts and feelings.

While part of me feels I've known you for ever, that there was never a time when I wasn't in love with you, there's another part of me that needs to know so much more about you, my beautiful Ellena.'

She sighed happily, and then concentrated really hard—but, instead of telling him anything, she found she was asking, 'That night, that night last week when you came home late from your business dinner, when you came into my room—it—er—wasn't in your mind to kiss me, was it?'

Gideon's mouth picked up at the corners. 'Not to start with. Having kissed you a couple of weeks before on my way out—knowing you'd think it was because Mrs Morris was around—I...'

'I remember that—we were in the hall. Mrs Morris wasn't...!' she gasped.

'She was nowhere near,' he confessed, not looking the slightest ashamed of himself. 'I kissed you purely because I was glad to see you, found that I didn't want to leave you, but, having done so, I realised that I was getting too attracted to you—and, since forward thinking decreed that was a no-no, I tried my level best to distance myself from you.'

Amazement mingled with pleasure because Gideon was being so wonderfully open with her, trusting in her love, revealing to her his innermost thoughts. 'I love you,' she said, purely because she had to, and was drawn up against his heart as he once more placed his mouth over hers.

'Keep telling me,' he insisted.

'Don't you believe me?'

'It's so utterly fantastic,' he answered jubilantly, and for long minutes was content to just hold her in his arms. Then he was saying ruefully, 'So there I was, thinking I might distance myself from you.'

'You couldn't?' she smiled impishly.

'Not always. There were times when I just couldn't resist your company. Which is why, lonesome for a sight of you, I came to your room that night and found you still working at your desk.'

'You came to tell me you would be away early the next morning,' Ellena remembered.

'And, for my sins, had to get up extra early so you wouldn't see that excuse for the lie it was.'

'It wasn't!' she gasped, and just had to burst out laughing. 'You lying toad!' she laughed. 'You wonderful, wonderful lying toad!' She pulled back to look at him and loved that he seemed to be enjoying her laughter, for his expression was clearly delighted.

'I hadn't seen you all day—I was missing you,' Gideon excused as her laughter faded.

'You—massaged my neck and shoulders,' she remembered. 'Er—did you have any idea of the—um—emotions you awakened in me that night?'

'Oh, sweet love,' Gideon said softly. 'I'm afraid I did suspect that you were not physically immune to me—just as you knew, I think, how very badly I wanted to kiss you.'

She sighed in pleasure. 'I thought you were going to, but then thought I'd got it wrong when you didn't.'

'Sweet Ellena, you got it absolutely right. I,' he went on to confess, 'got it absolutely wrong the next evening when, with you on my mind for most of that day, I'd just left a hotel conference room—and couldn't believe my eyes when through the glass doors of the dining room I saw you smiling happily at some good-looking swain as you ate your dinner.'

'You were jealous!' she gasped.

'I was furious! Damn that for a tale! I barely realised what I was doing when I charged through those doors, intent only on letting your good-looking escort know that you lived with me.'

'You *were* jealous!' she laughed.

'Wretched woman!' he becalled her. 'So I was jealous,' he admitted. 'As jealous as hell. I've never before known such a gut-tearing murderous emotion.'

Ellena was instantly contrite. 'I'm sorry. I should have phoned you to tell you about it in advance—only, well, I was still quite confused about what you'd made me feel the night before.'

'You say the most fantastic things,' he teased.

She looked away, shy for a brief moment. 'We had a row when I got home,' she recalled dreamily.

'Why wouldn't we?' he acknowledged. 'It was around midnight when you got home, and I'd been pacing the floor, alternating between concern for your safety and fury—jealousy blinding me to what I knew of you.'

'We did kiss and make up,' she reminded him.

'Oh, that we did,' he smiled.

'It seemed so right,' Ellena smiled back.

'It was,' he agreed. 'But I found you were so much on my mind, rarely out of my head, that I feared everything was getting out of hand. I felt I should calm the situation down—my study became my prison.'

'Serves you right,' she teased lovingly.

'It did too. Within a very few days we were having staffing problems and you were covering for them by having Violette sleep in your room. Which rather defeated the object,' *he* teased, 'when said infant started hollering—and you slept straight through it.'

'It was your fault,' she blamed him cheerfully. 'Thoughts of you kept me awake half the night! I'd only just dropped off when you were waking me up, a helpless male with a damp baby in your arms.'

'Remind me to get you for that!' he threatened. 'Though it's a fact I was wide awake with you on my mind when the little one started yelling. Did I mention, by the way, that you look adorable in sleep, with your hair all tousled and a beautiful tint of pink on your skin?'

'Oh, Gideon,' she murmured, and they kissed.

'Oh, my darling, I love you so much,' he breathed. And kissed her again, but pulled back to ask, 'When did you know for sure that you loved me?'

'In the early hours of yesterday morning,' she answered without hesitation. 'We got Violette settled to sleep again. And somehow started to make love—and I just knew. I no longer had to wonder why it was that you kept me sleepless. It was just—there. I knew I was in love with you.'

'Oh, sweet, sweet Ellena,' he breathed, and softly asked, 'Was that after you heartlessly informed me that you didn't think our making love was a very good idea?'

'I didn't mean to be heartless,' she said at once. But, remembering everything about that night, and with the honesty which Gideon appreciated, she mentioned slowly, 'I don't think I've ever felt so sensitive as I did at that particular time.'

'Entirely understandable, my little love,' Gideon murmured.

'You called me sweetheart,' she reminded him. 'Only you'd done it before—but for Mrs Morris's benefit—you'd meant nothing by it. And…'

'Oh, darling—in your highly sensitive state you thought I meant nothing by the endearment then?' Gideon cut in tenderly. 'You thought our lovemaking meant nothing to me! Sweet love,' he added gently, 'I loved you then, as I love you now.'

They kissed away any traces of pain or anguish. 'I'm sorry,' she apologised lovingly as they pulled back to look at each other.

'What for?' he teased, clearly having forgiven her for every one of her misdeeds.

'For being as outraged and jealous as you, for one thing,' she smiled.

'This I want to hear,' he encouraged.

'Last night—at that hotel,' she reminded him.

'Yes?' hc quite plainly wanted more.

'I'd popped in to return some books they wanted—they're clients,' she inserted. 'And there are you, absolutely totally absorbed with a beautiful brunette... Need I go on?'

'The detective saw at once what I failed to see,' Gideon answered, cheerfully reminiscent.

'She saw I was in love with you,' Ellena agreed, confessing, 'I was appalled by my behaviour afterwards.'

'And I didn't know where the devil I was,' he owned. 'All the while I was wondering, dismissing, and hoping, that Mrs Turner had got it right when she stated ''Now there's a lady in love'', clearly meaning in love with me. At the same time I was trying to keep a lid on the hope she had given me about that phone call from Spain to the hotel in Austria from Señora Pender.'

'You intended to tell me about it when you came home and came to my room, didn't you?'

'There were so many reasons why I came to your room last night,' he owned. 'With Mrs Turner being certain you loved me, it was a splendid excuse—it wouldn't wait until morning—to try and find out how you felt personally about me. Also, I'd kept to myself the information I had that a couple answering Kit and Justine's description had left the area before the avalanche had struck. It had seemed to me too cruel to raise your hopes on anything so vague when the ski resort must have hundreds of couples who would fit the same description. But this time, backed by your absolute faith that Justine would never leave a hotel bill unpaid, I felt I had to share this latest news with you.'

'But—you didn't,' she teased. With both Justine and Kit now safe—not to mention that the man she loved incredibly loved her back— Ellena had no trouble in feeling light-hearted.

'I was nervous,' Gideon admitted. 'Afraid of tripping over my words, and not knowing what to do first—tell you of the news from Austria, or try to find out if there was a chance that our detective might have got it right and you did care for me. You were not,' he accused, 'at all as I would imagine you would be—if you loved me.'

'Well—er—not to start with,' she agreed, feeling a shade pink about the cheeks. 'But I didn't know then that you loved me. If I remember rightly, you weren't too lover-like yourself to start with.'

'Why would I be? I'd come to your room with a head and heart full of matters that wouldn't wait until morning, and there you were sounding more as though you hated me than loved me. And if that wasn't enough, when I came home filled with hope, you had the colossal nerve to start talking divorce lawyers!'

'You—er—did seem a bit angry about that,' she murmured demurely.

'Wretch! I was furious!' Gideon admitted wryly.

'We did kiss and make each other better,' Ellena reminded him quickly.

'What was better about you so beautifully sending me away to my own bed?' he demanded mock-severely.

'I—was—um—frightened you'd think me gauche, might be disappointed that I didn't know very much,' Ellena confessed—and could only wonder at the tenderness for her that came over his expression.

'Oh, little love, your innocence is precious, didn't you know that?' he murmured gently. And, finding himself at fault, not her, he said, 'I should have been more understanding.'

'Don't say that! You were. You were understanding! You were wonderful. Only...'

'Only?' he encouraged.

'Only you referred to the night before when you asked was I going to go all bad-mannered on you again? And...'

'Oh, love, my sensitive love—and you remembered I'd called you sweetheart the previous evening, and you believed again our love-making meant nothing to me.'

'You called me sweetheart once more on your way out.'

'Oh, little darling! Are you going to forgive me my sins?'

'Every one of them,' she smiled, and tenderly they kissed.

'What a woman you are!' he murmured adoringly, when after their tender kiss they drew apart and just looked lovingly at each other. 'Is it any wonder you come between me and my work, me and my sleep?'

'You were awake early this morning—I heard you moving about.'

'You were awake too?' Ellena gave a small nod, and Gideon cradled her into his shoulder. 'How could I sleep with so much going on in my head? I'd hoped to have some kind of a conversation with you this morning, even imagined that you might feel a little shy of me. I was all ready to put you at your ease. But no, even though you blushed scarlet, you didn't give me the chance to try and make things easier. You appeared to let me know you hadn't given me so much as another thought; in you breezed to the breakfast room as bright as a button, not interested in breakfast, and certainly not seeming to give a damn about me in your rush to get to your infernal pending file.'

'It would seem that love makes liars of us all,' she confessed, and apologised, 'It was the only way I could think of facing you after... Anyhow, it wasn't long before I saw you again.' She smiled. 'You came to my office to take me to the airport.'

'That was one hell of a wait!'

'I wouldn't argue that,' Ellena replied. 'Can you imagine Pamela withholding the information that Justine had been in touch!'

'I should have realised what she was up to—but just didn't,' Gideon replied. 'It's just so unthinkable that anyone wouldn't have the common decency to pass that information on, that I never for a moment gave the notion a thought. She couldn't have told Russell either.'

'He'd have phoned?'

'Straight away. He may wear blinkers where his wife is concerned, but he knew I'd been worried.' For a moment, a whisper of bleakness crossed his expression, and Ellena knew that while she had kept her feelings and fears that she might never see Justine again bottled up and hidden, so, too, had Gideon.

'They're safe,' she said gently, and smiled at him. 'It's all over now,' she added softly.

'It isn't—is it?' Gideon asked, his expression serious, something new there in his question.

'I—don't think I'm with you?'

'Us!' he said distinctly. 'I mean us, Ellena.'

Us! Suddenly her heart was once more thundering against her ribs. She swallowed, and took a gulp of breath. 'What are you saying, Gideon?' she asked.

'I'm saying that, having said I would see you at Oakvale, I never dreamed you wouldn't be there when I got back. I'm saying that I was only a little relieved when I checked your wardrobes and found that your clothes were still there.'

'You rang and said the weekend would be fine for me to come and pick them up.'

'There was no way, sweet love, I was going to leave it until the weekend before I saw you again,' he smiled, and, placing a tender kiss on one corner of her mouth, 'Darling Ellena, the house is empty without you there.'

It was no use, she had to swallow again. 'You—um—could only have been there for a couple of minutes before you left Oakvale to come here,' she managed huskily.

'The ache for you, the fear in me that you wouldn't want to come back, was such that it was as though you had been away months.'

'You—want me to come back?' she whispered.

'My darling, I love you. You can't begin to know how much. Nor know how terrified I've been, and am, that my worst fears may be confirmed, and that you will not want to return. That you may, God forbid, want our marriage to be over.'

Ellena stared at him, her lovely eyes huge in her face. 'Are you saying—that—er—you don't?' she whispered.

'Sweet, sweet love,' he murmured. 'That's what I thought I'd been telling you all this while. That I love and adore you, and that I want you and I—us—to stay married—permanently.'

'Oh!' she exclaimed, her heartbeats racing, emotional tears of the moment not far away, making it impossible for her to say more.

'Will you, my darling?' Gideon asked, his tone growing urgent. 'Will you? Do you love me enough to come with me, and live with me, and be my wife?'

Ellena had to swallow one more time before she could speak. 'Oh, Gideon,' she answered chokily, 'I love you enough.'

She felt his arms tighten around her. 'You'll stay married to me—never to divorce?'

Unbelievably, he still sounded unsure! 'Oh, Gideon, don't you know? I love you so much—I never want to be apart from you.'

His exclamation was lost as he held her close to him, his face in her hair—and for long moments they stayed like that. Then he was getting to his feet, bringing her to her feet, standing there with his arms still around her.

'Are you ready, then, wife, to come home?' he asked gruffly.

Ellena beamed a smile at him, thoroughly enchanted. 'Yes, husband, I am,' she whispered rapturously.

There was time for just one more kiss before they went.

MILLS & BOON® PUBLISH EIGHT
LARGE PRINT TITLES A MONTH.
THESE ARE THE EIGHT TITLES
FOR OCTOBER 1998

THE MARRIAGE CAMPAIGN
Helen Bianchin

INHERITED: ONE NANNY
Emma Darcy

THE FOREVER AFFAIR
Catherine George

MARRIED TO A MISTRESS
Lynne Graham

MARRIED IN A MOMENT
Jessica Steele

THE IMPATIENT VIRGIN
Anne Weale

MISSION TO SEDUCE
Sally Wentworth

CATCHING KATIE
Sophie Weston

MILLS & BOON® PUBLISH EIGHT
LARGE PRINT TITLES A MONTH.
THESE ARE THE EIGHT TITLES
FOR NOVEMBER 1998

IN BED WITH A STRANGER
Lindsay Armstrong

FORBIDDEN PLEASURE
Robyn Donald

A HUSBAND'S PRICE
Diana Hamilton

THE TWENTY-FOUR-HOUR BRIDE
Day Leclaire

JOINED BY MARRIAGE
Carole Mortimer

NANNY BY CHANCE
Betty Neels

THE MARRIAGE SURRENDER
Michelle Reid

GABRIEL'S MISSION
Margaret Way